To Ben

Enjoy

Books by TLW Savage

First Test Quartet

Alex Twice Abducted
Alex Terrified Hero
Alex Inner Voice
Alex and the Crystal of Jedh....Not published as of March 2019

Dark Universe Series

Alex Twice Abducted

TLW Savage

Pronunciations

- A'idah – Ī ē duh

  Twelve year old girl from Northwest Pakistan, one of Alex's best friends and a member of his flock

- Amable – Ă muh bull

  The leader of the aliens abducting and training the Earthlings

- Coruscated – kor uh skāt ed

  Definition: *flashed or sparkled*

- Ekbal – ĕhk bal

  Twelve year old boy from southern India, a member of Alex's flock

- Gaahr – Gahr; simply ah with a hard g sound in front followed by the rrr sound

  A species of deem

- Gagugugul – Gah goo goo gull

  A Gaahr

- Gursha – Ger shuh

  The nurse for Alex's flock

- Haal - Hăl

  A dwarf

- Heyeze – Hī ēz

  An evil philosopher of the dolphins

- Hheilea – Hī lē uh

  A kimley fifteen year old girl

- Hhy Soaley – Hī sōl ē

  Hheilea in disguise as a boy

- Hymeron – Hī mer uhn

  Hheilea's brother

- Lepercaul – lĕp r call

  An alien specie

- Lillyputi – lĭl ē poo tē

  A wonderful desert, which is dangerously addictive for humans

- Maleky – Muh lĕk ē

  The most evil person in the galaxy

- Numbel – Nuhm bell

  A dwarf

- Osamu – ō săm oo: the oo is the same sound in boo

  A Japanese man and a member of Alex's flock

- Sabu – Să boo

  A snow leopard and a member of Alex's flock

- Skyler – skī ler

  A Blue Hyacinth Macaw and a member of Alex's flock

- Tierce – tirs; pronounced like tear plus a c sound like in pierce

  A fencing term referring to a type of block

- Twarbie – twăr bē

  A winkle female, who looks like she might be close to Alex's age

- Vapuc – vă pook

  The result of dark matter affecting a living creature to allow it to alter the laws of the universe

- Ytell – yuh tĕl

  A raptor, who is the leader of Alex's flock and the leader of the other raptors

- Zeghes –zā s

  A six month old dolphin who is a member of Alex's flock

DEDICATION

This book's dedicated to my fans and many more: Porsche Appleman, my first fan and a wonderful fan, may all my future fans be just as fanatical; to my two daughters, Lynn and Laura, who first suggested I write stories for others to read and enjoy; and to my wonderful wife, Debbie, her forbearance for years with my writing struggles allowed for the opportunity to continue to fruition. All of your support and belief in me and in this project has been instrumental in its success.

This book wouldn't exist without the hard work and sincere efforts of Porsche Appleman, Laurie Rosin, Irene Roth Luvaul, Judy Walker, and Debbie Walker. The hundreds of hours you spent laboring with me were appreciated more than you'll ever know.

A very special thanks to a local author, Connie Jasperson, who has been there for me as a volunteer editor, fan, friend, and mentor.

I want to thank the many who helped me with the research. The Kalasha researcher, Wynne Maggi, for her invaluable help in understanding the Kalasha people. Lee Merrick of Alaska Falcons helped me to get the characterization of Ytell and the other alien raptors right. When I'm writing of the alien raptors I think of his beautiful Gyrfalcons.

Then there are the countless many who patiently listened to me talk about it and read portions to give me feedback. You know who you are and I hope you find those who'll help you with your dreams.

Last, but not least is a great thanks to Laura for helping me finish this project.

What follows is the best thanks I can give, please read on, laugh, cry, think, be amazed, fascinated and enjoy.

CONTENTS

Chapter One
Alien Abduction

Unconscious, Alex lay alone in the wet grass. Fog swirled around him. For a year he'd been fighting the inevitable. The doctors had said he was dying of unknown causes, but today for the first time his illness took a back seat. The lack of control over his life wasn't new, but the strangeness was.

The sound of sirens drew Alex back to consciousness. He opened his eyes to fog. Frantic, he tried to get up, but he couldn't move his body. A scream burst from him. "Aah! Help!" The sirens came closer.

A man called out, "Who's out there?!"

"Over here! Help me!"

"Keep shouting," the man said. "This strange fog is making it hard to find you."

The ground fell away from under him. Misty tendrils of fog streamed past. Sunshine struck his face. Blinded by the light, scared, and confused, one thought screamed in his mind. *I'm being abducted.* Something above him drew nearer, and then it blocked the sun. Alex was pulled up into the object and through a tube. Lights flashed quickly by until he popped from the tube.

A cacophony of sounds assaulted him as his body settled onto a large, yellow disc. A sharp pungent smell, like ozone, assailed his nose, and he sneezed. After rolling over, Alex struggled to his knees. A shimmering wall of yellow light rose from the edge of his disc. Placing his hand on the wall of light he felt it give a little, before hardening. Other discs of different colors with their own walls, prisons of light, floated around him. Each prison held a person or animal. Above the disc nearest Alex, a dolphin somehow floated and moved in the air, and they stared at each other. *What does it think of being captured, and given the ability to move in the air, like it's water?*

~**********~

Zeghes whistled and twisted in the air. The new two-legged looked at him, and Zeghes looked intently back. *He's a male and ill. I need to get to him. Sick shouldn't be by themselves.* Zeghes rammed the wall of light again and again, trying to get out. *One of these big birds might decide to eat the boy. I have to protect him.*

As Zeghes fought, the boy left his disc with a white-haired creature's help. From above came loud, piercing calls. *I don't think they're happy about the boy getting out of his prison.* One of the raptors launched from a perch to dive toward the boy. *The bird's going to attack. I need to get free.* Zeghes battered himself against the wall of light, ignoring the pain, until darkness swallowed up his awareness.

Chapter Two
Zeghes and A'idah get to know Alex

Zeghes, the dolphin, swam through the air. He didn't need the small, bouncing ball of light guiding them, because he'd created a map in his head of this part of the labyrinth of halls. From behind him came the echoing sounds of A'idah's footsteps. The changes in the last five days overwhelmed him. He could understand what everyone said, including the aliens. Zeghes didn't know if he could trust them, even though the aliens kept saying: we are trying to help you. The aliens were helping the boy, Alex. Zeghes also loved the transparent suit the aliens gave him. From behind him, A'idah said, "Wait up. I have to see him first."

Zeghes twisted back in the air to face her. "Stop trying to tell me what to do. Girls aren't supposed to order guys about."

A'idah ducked past him to enter the nurses' clinic. "Get used to it, Zeghes. I'm not a dolphin."

Gursha, the four-armed nurse greeted them, "You're just in time." She turned to Alex. "Alex, wake-up. Some of your flock members are here to meet you."

Alex lay surrounded by a blue haze, except for the pink haze around his head. He floated in the haze about three feet off the ground. Alex blinked and turned his head toward them.

"Hi there, Alex," Zeghes said. "Don't worry about any danger. Zeghes is here. That's me. The girl is A'idah. You go ahead and talk to her. I'm going to patrol the area for sharks."

"Uh, hi," Alex said weakly. "There was another dream before this." He paused and then said, "I slugged a giant bird."

"Hi," A'idah said and turned to Gursha. "Are you sure he's ready for company?"

3

"He's just a bit groggy. He needs to get up for a while."

Zeghes had paused for a moment, as he listened to the conversation, before he swam away to patrol.

"I like this dream. It's better than the ..." Alex's words faded as Zeghes moved farther from the clinic. Moving his head back and forth, he built a map in his head of the passageways as he swam. *It's kinda like a coral reef without water.* A semi-translucent creature, eight-feet tall and four-feet wide, waddled around a corner of the passageway. Zeghes said, "You need to scoot over to make room for me to get by."

The creature lifted a thick arm and pointed at Zeghes. "You're one of the new Earthlings. I don't scoot over."

Then the creature waved a hand, and Zeghes found himself pushed against the ceiling, as below the creature started to thump past. Zeghes remembered using a similar type of force to shove a shark out of the water, back on Earth, before the aliens abducted him. He shoved back at the creature, pushing him down onto the floor. Immediately, Zeghes swam back toward the clinic. *I don't think all of these aliens are very nice. It's just like in the ocean. Some dolphins are bullies too.* He remembered hearing stories about dolphins across the ocean killing porpoises just for the fun of it. As he approached the clinic, A'idah's voice roused him from his own thoughts.

"You froze water and made yourself lighter?" She said.

"I guess so."

Zeghes swam back into the room. *That must've been Alex.* "All safe. No sharks."

Alex stood beside A'idah, wearing cream-colored, loose pants and shirt like the other humans, and he said, "A dolphin, right here, in the air. He's swimming in the air and talking to me."

"He's been given some kind of fancy suit," A'idah said as she smiled at Alex. "It makes him able to swim through the air just like he's still in the water."

"What makes him able to talk?" Alex asked.

A'idah pointed toward her ear. "I guess you haven't heard about squirts yet."

"What're squirts?"

"Small organisms placed behind our ears. They make it so we can understand the animals and the aliens," A'idah said.

Alex's hand started to move up to his ear. "This is crazy. Are there really sharks up here?"

"On Earth, we always watch for sharks," Zeghes said. "I'm told there are no sharks here. But I still watch." *Especially the raptors, they seem like a shark.*

"Can I touch you?" Alex asked Zeghes.

"Sure thing."

"I can feel the suit you're wearing, and yet it lets my hand through to touch your skin. This is amazing. Gursha says I'm going to live and ..." Tears cascaded down his face. Zeghes rubbed against him.

A'idah put her arms around Zeghes and Alex. "Hey, I understand. I bawled like a baby after I began to move and feel again."

"Thanks for holding me," Alex said, straightening up and sniffing. "Sorry I lost it."

Zeghes had watched two white-haired creatures, similar to the humans, sneak into the clinic, and now they ran out of the room.

A'idah looked down at her feet and then at Alex's feet. "Wait!"

She spoke too late. Alex started to take a step. "When did those —?" He tipped forward, thin arms windmilling, and grabbed for A'idah. Missing, he fell down. "Ah!"

Laughing, A'idah said, "Sorry for laughing about your shoes being tied together. The Soaley boys seem to victimize everyone. They're kimleys, one of the many different kinds of aliens you're going to meet."

Zeghes backed up, looking after the kimleys. *I saw one of those creatures the first day, but A'idah called them both boys. It's probably just another thing I'm confused about here.*

The sound of heavy footsteps came from the doorway. Zeghes turned to see Ytell, a dark blue, almost black raptor entering the clinic. A'idah stepped between Alex and Ytell, craned her neck to look up at Ytell's face, and said, "You came too soon."

5

"Look out, A'idah," Alex said, scrambling to his feet. "It's the alien that bit me."

Ytell tipped his head to consider A'idah with one yellow and red eye. "I'm sorry. Haven't you explained to Alex what's going on?"

It's the shark. Zeghes dove at Ytell. Too late he saw Ytell's hooked beak slash down at him, but the beak stopped just before cutting into him. Zeghes rammed into Ytell. "You need to leave Alex alone. He's still sick. You can't catch us and shove us around like you do. It isn't right."

Ytell backed up, and Zeghes hung in the air. Confusion surfaced as Zeghes realized Ytell had chosen not to defend himself. He moved his head back and forth, examining Ytell with his sonar. He could see broken ribs. *Why's the shark standing still?* Meanwhile, Alex and A'idah both spoke at the same time.

A'idah poked at Ytell's dark-red breast with her finger. "Zeghes is right. You need to leave Alex alone. We're informing him about what's going on."

Alex hopped forward. "Don't hurt my friend," he said falling against A'idah, taking both of them down onto Ytell's scaly, blue feet.

Gursha bustled forward, and Zeghes drifted out of her way. Her voice resonated with authority and irritation. "You Earthlings be quiet and wait. Ytell, you're hurt. Come over here."

Shaking his head, Ytell pulled his feet out from under the two humans. "I can—"

Gursha interrupted him with a glare and pointed to a pattern on the floor. After taking a step Ytell paused, and shuffled the rest of the way to the pattern.

A blue haze rose up lifting Ytell. It turned pink around the area Zeghes had hit. Gursha muttered to herself, one set of hands on her hips and with the other set reached into the haze. "You didn't have to let him break your ribs."

Ytell said, "Zeghes could've gotten hurt, and fighting with him would slow down his acclimatization. We've already caused him trouble adjusting. He thinks I'm the equivalent of a shark. For Earth's sake all of the Earthlings must progress

6

e

quickly."

Gursha pulled her hands out of the haze as some of the pink turned to blue. "Okay, your ribs have begun to knit. I don't suppose you'll stay until they're completely mended?"

"No."

The blue haze faded away, lowering Ytell to the ground. He stretched and slightly opened his wings. Shaking his feathers, he closed his wings back against his body. Gursha frowned and stepped closer to him. "Don't fly during the next few days and come back if it starts hurting again."

"Thank you," Ytell said.

Gursha said, "Of course you won't come back because of a little pain, you stubborn bird, and since you're too stubborn to stay until you're healed, you need to leave. This has been too much excitement for my other patient."

Ytell turned to Alex. "I'm Ytell, your flock leader. I'll see you tomorrow morning." Then he left with a swish of his feathers.

Watching in confusion, Zeghes had a new thought coalesce about Ytell. Maybe Ytell is like the dominant dolphins and not a shark. Except the big male dolphins wouldn't have let Zeghes get away with ramming one of them. Even the females wouldn't have let him. Zeghes looked at the two humans. A'idah and Alex were still on the floor, watching as Ytell left.

A'idah laughed a short nervous laugh and said, "We showed him."

A grin replaced the scowl on Alex's face, as he joined A'idah in laughter. "I guess we did."

Gursha came over, and helped Alex and then A'idah back on their feet. When Alex stood on his feet again, he said, "Thanks, Gursha."

Gursha continued to hold A'idah by the arm, and spoke to Alex. "Do you see that pattern on the floor?"

"Yes."

"Go sit down in the air over it. The holo field will respond to your thoughts and support you."

"Okay." Alex turned around and awkwardly sat in midair. A blue haze appeared around his body, supporting him in a sitting position. "What did Ytell mean about causing Zeghes trouble?"

A'idah tried to pull away from Gursha, and said, "After Zeghes was torn from his pod in the abduction, he saw you fight Ytell, one of the abductors. That caused him to bond with you and me as his new pod which means we're his family. However it also caused his aggression towards Ytell. He has Ytell confused with his idea of sharks. The PETA rep says Ytell has to allow it, per a signed agreement. She says Zeghes will eventually heal from the abduction trauma, and the aggression toward Ytell will stop."

Zeghes started to speak and then changed his mind, as he tried to sort out what he'd just heard.

Alex said, "So now you, Zeghes, and I are family? I like that idea. I'll try and be a good big brother, for him and you."

Gursha shook A'idah by the arm she held. "A'idah?"

"What?" A'idah tried again to pull away.

"Young lady," Gursha said, glowering at A'idah. "You forget your responsibility to Alex. We talked about this during your visits here."

Alex looked back and forth between the two of them. A'idah opened her mouth to reply, but Gursha held up a hand, keeping two firmly on her hips. "Don't excuse yourself to me. Tell Alex what he needs to know."

A'idah looked at Alex and then down at his feet. "I'm sorry, I should've talked about this before Ytell arrived. I told him I would."

"What?" Alex asked.

"Get on with it," Gursha said.

A'idah looked up into Alex's eyes. "I knew Ytell was just coming to talk to you. He has checked up on you every day. He's been concerned about your health. Also, he wasn't attacking you on the day of your abduction and he won't attack you now. They needed to finish sorting out the flocks, and Alex, you were holding things up. They couldn't leave Earth until they finished. Ytell is worried about having enough time to help us. We must accomplish something before the year is up, or the aliens will give up on Earth. Which would mean everyone on Earth dies."

A'idah paused, breathing deep, and her eyes glistened. Gursha pulled her close. "If you had said that sooner, Alex wouldn't have reacted to Ytell the way he did, which might've kept Zeghes from attacking Ytell."

"I'm sorry ... for not telling him sooner," A'idah said.

"That's enough visiting for now. I want all of you out," Gursha said.

"I should stay with Alex," Zeghes said. "Sick pod members should not be left alone."

"He'll be fine, Zeghes," Gursha said.

A'idah paused at the door. "Thanks for standing up to Ytell for me, Alex."

Alex said, "Family have to stand up for each other, and don't worry about not having told me all that stuff before Ytell arrived. When I saw him again, I still would've reacted the same way."

Again, Zeghes wanted to speak up. He'd rammed Ytell. Why didn't A'idah thank him? Outside in the hall, he realized A'idah wasn't with him. Twisting around, he saw her standing still by the door of the clinic. Gliding back, he bumped A'idah. "What are you doing?"

A'idah looked at Zeghes for a moment before saying, "I don't want to leave, but I guess we'll see him tomorrow."

Chapter Three
Zeghes Saves Alex

The next day, Zeghes hurried ahead of the flock. Ahead of him the small bouncing ball of light sped up to keep pace with him. His sonar told him a huge space was at the end of the hall. Speeding faster he rocketed through a doorway and into the Hall of Flight. A vast open space greeted him. He hadn't realized how suffocating the tight confines of rooms and passageways had been. Joy filled him, and he did barrel rolls out into the middle of the huge room. In the distance, he could see other Raptors and their flocks. In his joy he didn't notice a voice calling to him.

"Zeghes! I said get back here!" Ytell yelled the second time.

Zeghes looked back to the entrance. The rest of his flock had gathered on the balcony there, and he went over their names in his head. Sabu, a snow leopard, chased after Skyler, a blue hyacinth macaw, as the bird flew just out of her paw's reach. Ekbal, a dark-skinned boy, squatted on the ground examining something. Alex and A'idah stood together by the doorway. Peter, the flock's skeptic, stood with arms crossed, scowling. The last member stood close to Ytell. He was an older, human man called Osamu, and his look back at Zeghes chased away all of Zeghes' good feelings. Osamu ordered all the nonhuman Earthlings around, and worse, he had eaten dolphin meat in the past. Zeghes slapped at the air with his tail in annoyance and swam back toward the flock. As he soared closer, he heard Ytell start another boring lecture. "The green areas with yellow circles are bubble platforms. Everyone find a circle to stand on. That goes for you too, Zeghes. Just float over one."

Ytell nodded in approval at the flock members. "Stay still until the bubble forms. These are special bubbles used to determine the individual's ability to react to Dark Matter. The more you react to Dark Matter, the better you will be able to control the movement of your bubble with your thoughts. Not everyone can use these bubbles, but anyone can use normal bubbles."

"What's the red circle?" Ekbal asked.

"It's broken," Ytell answered.

Zeghes saw bubbles growing up from the circles to surround each flock member. *What is that odd tingling sensation?* Looking down, he saw a bubble rapidly encase him.

The bubbles had an iridescent sheen, just like soap bubbles. Zeghes soared into the middle of the hall in his bubble. Others floated up and moved slowly away. Shouting interrupted the scene and drew his attention.

Peter pushed at the wall of his bubble. "Protect me from this evil, Lord! Keep these demons from me! With thy power, these demons have no control over me!"

Over the yelling came Ytell's firm voice, "You have been identified as someone, who through a natural force, not a spiritual force, does many things mostly unexplained by our science. I don't have time to waste. This will prove if Dark Matter affects you."

With that, Ytell partially opened his wings, which then spanned twenty feet. A mighty beat of his wings caused a gust of air to push Peter's bubble over the edge of the platform, and it fell. Everyone heard a short scream. A moment later, Peter in his bubble rocketed back up.

"What have you done to me?" Peter sobbed. "I thought you were interested in what I told you about God, but then you did this."

"I was intrigued about what you said, but you need to listen me," Ytell said.

The rest of the flock bobbled, soared, or at least gently moved through the air in their bubbles, except for Alex.

"It's easy. Just make your bubble move," Osamu said. "It

responds to your thoughts."

"Come on, Alex. It's fun," A'idah said.

Zeghes moved closer to Alex. *Something's not right.* Alex jumped up and down, and his bubble moved a little. He charged forward in his bubble and off the edge. His bubble fell toward the distant floor.

"Ahhh!" Alex screamed.

Zeghes in his bubble dashed below Alex and bounced into his bubble causing it to rise. He continued bumping into Alex's bubble until finally Alex's bubble bounced back onto the platform and dissipated, leaving him sprawled on the ground at Ytell's feet.

Zeghes spun in his bubble. *This is fun. I liked saving Alex.*

Turning to Alex, Ytell said, "Go stand out of the way by the entrance." And then he looked at Zeghes. "Thanks. If necessary, I would've caught Alex, but you used great initiative."

"No! I'm trying again," Alex said.

"Alex." Ytell leaned his head down toward him. "Fighting with me is a waste of our time."

"I'll teach you to spin me." Skyler's voice came from the middle of the hall snatching Zeghes' attention. He turned to see Sabu had just spun Skyler's bubble with a swat from a magically enlarged paw. It made Zeghes think of the rough games he played with the other young dolphins. As everyone watched, Skyler let Sabu close in behind him. It became evident he could move faster as he rolled up and over, coming down right behind Sabu.

With a "See how you like this," Skyler clamped onto Sabu's bubble with what looked like an incredibly large bill and shook it.

Ytell said, "Everyone look at those two. They're using an innate ability to do two forms of *vapuc*, illusion and force. Vapuc is not magic or a spiritual force of any kind. Vapuc is what we call the things you can do if you react to Dark Matter. When we get to the academy, you'll learn how force works. How they made the enlarged bill and paw appear still puzzles us."

Next, Zeghes heard Ytell scolding Alex, "I told you to go

back to the entrance."

Alex said in an accusatory tone, "You got rid of my bubble."

"I don't have time to figure out what's going on with you. Go stand by the wall."

Zeghes wanted to go play, but he couldn't leave Alex. He could tell Alex wasn't happy and maybe even ill. Peter drifted through the air to Alex. "You're a lucky one, Alex. This evil has no grip on you." His voice rose. "I pray for my own release from this foul situation."

Alex stepped toward Peter. "But this is a chance for us to help other people."

"How can you trust what these aliens say? You're a child. How can you understand? I'm a preacher, a man of God. I know what's right and wrong."

Zeghes soared towards Alex and Peter. "Leave him alone! You sound like Heyeze. He led many of my people to their death. He tried to tell them he was the source of truth, but he knew nothing. He was evil. I don't know much, but claiming you know what's right and wrong is just like Heyeze."

"Ha," Peter said. "Animals don't have philosophers. You're lying."

Zeghes charged Peter's bubble and yelled, "Begone." With a shriek that faded in the distance, Peter's bubble ricocheted about the hall.

A'idah came up to them. "Good job, Zeghes. The other humans need to respect everyone. Hang in there, Alex. We'll get this figured out."

As others gathered by Alex, Ytell said, "Zeghes, I understand why you attacked Peter, but we can't fight each other. Consider this your only warning. If you fight with each other, a device called a civilization band will be put on you. If you try to fight with the band on, it will knock you unconscious. Now, everyone head back to our common room. I'll meet you there."

Osamu said, "Ship, please give us a guide back to our rooms."

A ball of light materialized in front of the flock and bounced through the air toward the doorway they had come through earlier. Zeghes puzzled over Ytell's words as he followed the flock and listened to the conversations. *I remember fighting in the pod. It was how everyone knew their place. What do we do instead of fighting? If I learn how to fit in here, will I be able to fit in back in my pod? It's like the physical abduction was just the beginning of a process.*

Osamu walked between A'idah and Alex. "Do not worry about the bubbles back there. These aliens will figure out what's wrong."

"This is an incredible place," Alex said, as he looked at Osamu. "I hope I don't get sent back to Earth."

Osamu patted Alex on the back. "I remember you telling us about saving the kittens. I know you react to Dark Matter. The aliens on this ship would not make a mistake."

"Maybe my saving the kittens was a one-time shot."

"Stop questioning yourself," Osamu said.

Starting to hobble, A'idah took Alex's hand. "It doesn't matter if you react to Dark Matter or not. It doesn't change who you are. They better not try to send you back. I'll refuse to stay. They can lock me up in a cage or torture me. It won't do them any good."

Zeghes nudged A'idah with his bill. "You're limping. We need to get you back to Gursha, so she can help you finish healing."

Skyler came flapping and dodging past them. "What a crazy flock this is. Flocks have to work together to survive. I need food. I'm so hungry."

Alex said, "A'idah, what's wrong? I thought you were cured."

"Gursha told me it will take a while for the nerves in my brain to fully heal. Until then, I have to put up with this whenever I do too much exercise."

As they arrived at their common room, two stocky people and one of the kimley kids each pushing a cart loaded with food, came into the room, from the other side. Zeghes hadn't realized how hungry he was until he saw a huge ball of water filled with fish floating behind the last cart.

One of the short men with a black beard said, "You're back just in time to eat. We're still having problems getting your food requirements all figured out. Another flock suffered food poisoning yesterday. Hopefully, no one else gets poisoned because of problems with the food." He chuckled and pointed at his barrel chest. "I'm Numbel." He pointed to a bald man with a pointed, white beard. "The grumpy one over there's Haal, and our helper is Hhy. They will stay here to help with any problems."

A soft voice interjected, "Be careful with the fruit. I think someone goofed. It might be too spicy for you."

Zeghes looked over at the speaker. It was Hhy. And then he heard A'idah talking to Alex. "He's one of those troublesome Soaley boys. Come over here. How does this water float in the air?"

Zeghes turned his head to examine Hhy more closely with his sonar. *But A'idah said Hhy is a boy?*

Osamu stood examining the big ball of water with fish swimming in it. Tentatively, he poked at it and waved his hands under it. "I would like to know too."

Alex said, "In the space station, doesn't water make balls like this?"

Osamu looked appraisingly at Alex. "Yes, Alex. What are you thinking?"

"Well," Alex said. "We're on a space ship, and yet we're experiencing gravity. That means they must have technology to control gravity. Couldn't they make the area of the ball have no gravity?"

"I knew you could tell me how the aliens did this," A'idah said.

Osamu raised one eyebrow. "Very good, Alex. I think you are right. Oh, the things we will do on Earth with this technology."

Zeghes hung, perplexed in the air. *What are they talking about?* Ekbal's voice distracted him from his thought.

Ekbal said, "That fruit looks tempting to me." After gazing at it for a moment he walked over to the cart.

"Didn't you hear the fruit might be spicy?" Alex asked.

Ekbal paused, hand hovering over the fruit. "Yes, but the fruit looks so good." He took an orange and green-striped fruit and popped it into his mouth.

"Mmm this tastes good, not too hot." His face turned red, and tears streamed down his face. "Oh, hot! Water, water!"

Hhy snatched both a pitcher and a glass off a cart and hurried toward Ekbal who blundered about, waving his arms and calling for help.

Hhy ducked under one waving arm and dodged to the side. Ekbal blundered into the floating ball of water. Unfortunately, he tried to talk, and bubbles rose from his mouth. Gasping and choking, he ducked back out of the water. Hhy poured Ekbal a drink and slipped a slender arm around him to support him. After Ekbal's breathing steadied, he took the glass and gulped the liquid down.

"Thanks," Ekbal said to Hhy. "That fruit tasted wonderful. I wonder if a second one would be as painful."

Zeghes shifted his attention from one person to another. Sabu had retreated to a back corner, gnawing on something. Ekbal stood looking at the fruit and licking his lips. While everyone finished eating, Zeghes struggled with thoughts. *Everyone else is fitting in and beginning to understand new things, but I'm confused and just pretending to be comfortable with all of this.*

When Haal and Hhy started picking up after the meal, the flock jumped up, some to help, and some to eat a little more. Zeghes, had only eaten a few fish. His thoughts kept distracting him.

"Wait," Skyler said. "I want more nuts."

"You'll get too fat to fly," Sabu said and swatted playfully at Skyler's tail.

Skyler flapped away from him and knocked a bowl over, spilling its contents across the floor, as Ytell entered the room.

Seeing Ytell, Skyler said, "It was Sabu's fault. She swatted me."

Zeghes watched to see how Ytell would react. Ytell avoided looking at the bird. "Peter won't be coming back. Alex, come with me. We're going to Amable."

Zeghes looked back to Alex. *He's my pod member and still sick. I don't think he should go without me or A'idah, but how are sick people treated here?*

"Alex, we need to go," Ytell said, impatiently.

Turning around, Alex said, "Bye."

Zeghes leaped through the air, bumping Alex with his head. "Will he not come back? Shouldn't one of us go with him?"

A'idah hobbled to Alex and took his hand.

"A'idah and Zeghes, on my world your type of loyalty is greatly valued. Also, my world is a very harsh place. My people discard young who fail. Regardless of what the decision is, I will bring him back here. In the future I need all of you to trust me. My training methods will often seem like you are on your own, but I'll be watching out for you. You are my flock, if need be I would die for you."

"What?" Zeghes asked, as he looked around at the flock members for an answer. *How could they discard their young?*

Chapter Four
What will be done with Alex?

Meanwhile in Amable's office, Alex's fate was being discussed.

"No, no, no, we can't send Alex back to Earth," Amable said to Stick, a thin, six-foot-tall bald creature, the only other person in Amable's office. A faint tune recognizable as *Ode of Remembrance* emanated from the resting fish-plant.

Stick rubbed his chartreuse, bulbous forehead. "But he doesn't react to Dark Matter. He won't be able to do any types of vapuc. Keeping him for the next year is a waste of resources. Let me show you the figures."

"And I'm telling you, even if Alex doesn't react to Dark Matter, he'll be of use to the flock. If his flock develops as it should, they'll help deal with the threats to the academy. Alex's life will be in danger as a nonvapuc-able person, and his flock will have to learn to protect him," explained Amable. "That will be good for the flock, but I also hope we can find something Alex is good at."

"But sir, I checked with Gursha about Alex's sickness. She told me Alex isn't responding to treatment as he should. She doesn't think he'll recover from his illness. In fact, she suspects other aliens have done something to him. Alex could be part of Maleky's plan for Earth. It would be just the thing he would do."

Amable said, "Of course, Stick, and we can't forget the deception involved with Alex supposedly saving the kittens. He remembers saving the kittens, but he doesn't react to Dark Matter, except maybe sensing the future. Ergo, he couldn't have done vapuc in saving the kittens. Someone pulled off a

18

difficult trick to convince our team he reacted to Dark Matter. Someone wanted us to find Alex."

"It has to be Maleky," Stick said, wiping sweat off his forehead. "What are we going to do about Alex? I still think we should send him back to Earth."

Amable placed his arm around Stick. "There is an old saying: keep your friends close and your enemies closer. We are keeping Alex very close."

"Then you won't use the two Soaley kids to test him?"

"I don't see why not," Amable said.

"But we don't trust them either."

"That's true," Amable said. "Having Alex and the kids together will let us keep an eye on all of them at the same time."

"Alex seems like such a nice boy," Stick said sadly. "Wouldn't it be better to send him back to Earth? Might we ... have to ... kill him?"

"You're letting your emotions get in the way of your logic. If Alex is a tool of Maleky, sending him back to Earth would be a death sentence. I'm surprised at you for suggesting killing Alex. We don't kill people unless it is unavoidable to save others. Maleky destroys all of the tools that fail him. Besides, Mrs. Soaley took the rare action of sharing what she knew of the future, just to make sure we wouldn't miss Alex in our search of Earth for creatures that react to Dark Matter."

"We still trust the adult kimleys?" Stick asked.

"Yes, as much as we trust anyone."

"Then we continue with your plan for Alex?"

"Yes."

~**********~

Alex held onto A'idah's hand. *I don't want to leave.*

Zeghes glided right up to Ytell's beak. "I should go with Alex. He's still sick, and he might get abducted again."

Confused at his words, Alex looked at Zeghes. "How could I get abducted again?"

Zeghes hesitated and said, "Saying abduction was probably wrong. Our bodies were abducted the first time, but now, I feel like, who I am is being abducted. I mean ... since I've been here, I've changed, and I'll never be the same again. My self is being abducted. Who knows what these aliens will do to you?"

Ekbal came forward. "Wow, Zeghes. Dolphins do have philosophers"

A'idah said, "I think it's good to change. I'm looking forward to learning how to protect myself and others. But there's another type of abduction. Among my people, the Kalasha, I've seen older girls fall in love and get married. I think falling in love is a form of abduction, but Alex doesn't need to worry about it. How would he fall in love with an alien?"

Alex stood with his mouth open, as he tried to figure out what to say, but overwhelmed by thoughts. *Falling in love with an alien? Ew, that sounds gross and crazy. And why does Zeghes' concern about changing bother me?*

Ytell reached a long, thin arm out from under his feathers to grasp Alex. "Okay, enough with all the talk. We have to go."

As Ytell pulled Alex after him, the group said their farewells.

"Good luck, Alex."

"If you see some nuts, get some."

"Remember to believe in yourself."

"Don't show fear. That's when the sharks attack."

~**********~

Walking away from the flock, Alex tugged his arm away from the raptor. Ytell still felt quite alien to him, and feeling the scaly hand on his arm was unsettling. As they walked, he glanced at Ytell. "Would you really die for me?"

"Yes. For us raptors, it's a matter of honor."

"My Aunt Debbie died saving others. Dying so others can live is the greatest sacrifice."

"That's partly why Amable and all of us are fighting to save worlds from the deem. We are willing to give our lives for the battle."

After walking the nearly deserted halls with Ytell they

stopped before a door. They heard a "Come on in," as the door slid open. A strange man hurried over to Alex. His pink and violet hair had foot long tufts sticking out above his ears. He grasped Alex's hand and shook it vigorously. "Ah, here you are, Alex, a fine young man. I'm Amable, and the last time I saw you everyone was quite worried about you. It's wonderful to see you looking better. Obviously, Gursha has worked her miracles on you. How're you feeling?"

Alex choked back a laugh, as he gazed at the strange-looking man with large golden-brown eyes set in a pale face. Alex said, "Much better. It's been great getting healed. Gursha told me to come back again this—."

"She says you're doing great," Amable said, interrupting Alex. "She's going to check your progress and wants you to go through an exercise program. Your two personal trainers will meet you tomorrow. I've been so glad for how willing you are to do things. I presume you are willing to do this exercise program?"

Alex shrugged his shoulders. *What things? What's he talking about?* "I guess. What is it?"

"Just exercise," Amable said, starting to herd Alex and Ytell out of his office. "Glad you agreed to the program. The good news is you can rejoin your flock as soon as the training is over."

"Wait," Alex said. "Who are the trainers?"

"You'll meet them tomorrow," Amable said. "Goodbye."

And then the door shut in Alex's face. "Why wouldn't he answer me?" Alex asked Ytell.

Ytell squatted down to look Alex in the eye. "There's something he doesn't want to tell you. I'm sorry, but I don't know what it is."

Alex opened his mouth to respond and then shut it. *What do I say to this alien? How much are they not telling me or lying about?* "I better go see Gursha."

Ytell nodded his head. "And I better get back to the rest of the flock. No telling what's going on there."

For a moment Alex stood alone in the passageway, as the sound of Ytell's footsteps faded. *It's so quiet. Where's everyone?*

21

Remembering the instructions for moving about in the halls, he said, "Ship, please supply a guide to Gursha's clinic."

A bright bobbing light floated in the air and moved opposite the direction Ytell took, and then waited for him. Alex shrugged trying to get rid of his nervousness and started down the empty passageways toward the clinic. Minutes went by with one empty passageway after another, and then a misty green cloud floated around a corner. Alex stopped and stepped back, warily watching the cloud. His guide light bounced to a halt.

"It's okay, Earthling," a voice coming from the cloud said. "You don't need to be frightened."

"You didn't frighten me," Alex said lowering his hands and unclenching his fists. "I was just startled."

The cloud floated along the passageway toward Alex. He stepped to the side to let the cloud pass him. Just as the cloud drifted beside him, it suddenly oozed through the air at him. With a gasp, Alex flattened himself against the wall. Laughter filled the air, and then abruptly stopped. The cloud swirled in the air to face down the passageway, the direction Alex had come. It then backed up. A multitude of thoughts whirled in Alex's head. *It's just teasing me. How can it seem to face somewhere? I don't see any eyes.* A last thought made Alex both want to run and look down the passageway. *What frightened it?*

Alex looked down the hall to see a translucent creature roughly eight feet tall and four feet wide. It stomped on thick legs toward them. Each step caused shivers of movement through the massive body.

In an urgent tone, the cloud said to Alex, "Go on. I'll keep the baby lepercaul from hurting you."

For a moment Alex stood still. *A baby? This is a baby.*

The other creature spoke in a voice which was a strange combination of babyish, deep, and threatening. "I'm not a baby. And I just want to taste the Earthling. I've heard they're tasty. Ha-ha-ha, I wouldn't hurt him much. He-he-he-he."

Alex followed the cloud's advice and started walking down the passageway, trying not to run, as his guide light resumed moving. *Everything's going to be okay. I'm not scared.*

At first he continued to hear the conversation behind him. "You aren't supposed to be out here. You —"

"I can too. Hymeron has some fun for me."

Looking around with wide eyes, Alex walked faster and faster. Until eventually, he ran gasping into the clinic. Gursha's boisterous voice greeted him. "Hello, Alex. Is someone chasing you?"

Alex looked at her. *I'm going to be okay. I just need to keep it together and not show how frightened I am.* "No. I ... just didn't want to be late." *Deep breath and change the conversation.* "Where's all of your medical equipment?"

"The holo fields are my equipment," Gursha said. "Less advanced technologies use a confusing amount of unsanitary medical tools. It's a wonder everyone in your hospitals doesn't die from infections. Now, lie down in this holo field."

Alex smiled at Gursha and did as she asked. His view of the room turned pinkish as the haze of the holo field surrounded him.

"Why am I seeing some things pinkish?" Alex asked.

"Pink haze shows the areas of illness or problems. That is what's coloring your view of the room. Now, I'm going back to my office, and I want you to lie still."

Lying still, Alex started to think about the strange creatures he'd met in the halls. *The situation couldn't have been as bad as it seemed. Who's Hymeron?* Alex closed the door on those thoughts. *Everything's going to be okay.* Next his thoughts wandered to Hhy. Something about the boy puzzled him. *What was it?* Then thoughts of A'idah crowded Hhy out of his mind. He understood A'idah. *She's so .... I like spending time with her.* And then he laughed to himself. *I think I'm drawn to her because we're both human and she's a girl just a couple of years younger than me. I can't wait to see her again.*

At that thought, he remembered his dad and a conversation they had back before his parents died. Anguish rose up with the memory. "Son, you're becoming a teenager. You are going to have new feelings and urges. Eventually, you'll be drawn to girls. Be careful about letting the feelings and urges control you. You've seen the wonderful relationship your mom and I have. If you wait until you're older to get serious about a girl, then you can build a relationship like we have. Don't play with a girl's feelings. Treat her with respect. In your heart and mind, you'll know what's right. But it can be very difficult to do what's right. Know your mom and I'll always be there for you, and we'll be praying for you."

Except they aren't. Dad lied. Tears started to flow down Alex's cheeks. *I need their help. I miss them.*

At that moment, Gursha bustled in with Alex's dinner. "We're-Oh, Alex, what's wrong?" Gursha left the dinner to slip two hands under his shoulders, a third hand smoothed his hair back from his forehead, and the fourth hand held one of his hands.

Feeling like a baby, Alex leaned into Gursha. "I miss my folks."

"You'll see them in a year. We'll be taking you back for a visit."

"No. You don't understand. They're dead."

"Oh. Alex, it's good that you miss them. That means you love them. What do you believe about death?"

"My folks believed it was just a passage from this life to an eternal life."

Gursha looked into Alex's eyes. "What do you believe?"

"I don't know. When they died, I prayed to God, and I got comfort. But I don't really know what I believe."

"Alex, I've lost loved ones." Pausing to look away, Gursha added in a soft voice. "Too many." Taking a deep breath she looked back at Alex. "If you live life well, then you're going to lose people you care for, but if you never lived, then you never had them to lose. You have to find comfort in positive things that keep you living and giving. Be careful. There are things that will comfort, but they'll diminish you. The good kind of comfort keeps us strong in here." Gursha placed a hand over Alex's heart. "We have to be strong here to help those still living."

"Thanks, Gursha," Alex said.

"You can come to me with your problems anytime," Gursha said. "Now, we're making some progress with your cure. Your prescription is to eat, exercise, rest, and repeat."

24

"Repeat?" asked Alex.

"Keep doing those three things until I tell you to stop," Gursha said.

"You mean when this is done, I won't have to eat or rest?"

"You know what I mean," Gursha said with a laugh. "Now eat this food, and get to sleep. Tomorrow will be a busy day for you."

"How long before I'm totally cured?"

The holo field lifted Alex into a vertical position, and Gursha engulfed one of his hands with her large hand. "Alex, most of the fatigue is gone, but I'm having trouble getting rid of some problems. You and I will beat this. The uncertainty is part of the journey."

After Alex finished eating and as he drifted off to sleep, he heard her whispering to herself, "I hope Alex can defeat this evil inside him."

In the middle of the night Alex's hands groped for a non-existent weapon. His eyes popped open, and he looked around Gursha's barren clinic in the dim light. A dream about battling evil inside him still felt so real. He remembered his disappointment the evening before, when Gursha told him he was going to have to fight the illness for a while longer. Trying to force himself to feel better, he daydreamed about Zeghes and A'idah giving him his training. All the time, he wanted and hoped to fall back asleep and have better dreams. His worry about the illness morphed into wondering who or what would be training him. *I don't know any of these aliens, and I can't imagine understanding just how strange some of them are.*

Finally his body relaxed and he drifted back off to sleep. In the morning, Alex's eyelids fluttered in his sleep. A smile tugged at his mouth. A flowery fragrance drifted about on a breeze blowing across a meadow filled with strange and yet beautiful plants. A figure stepped out of dark evergreens bordering the meadow and walked slowly toward him. She wore a brown robe and her long light-brown hair danced in the breeze. Streaks of gold and red hair twinkled in the sunlight. She raised her face and he saw dark eyes with long curly eyelashes. Leisurely she swayed closer to him. The red of her lips caught his attention as the full lips slowly curved into a smile. Alex's heart beat faster and he stepped forward. Then she demurely ducked her head to the side. A slender hand covered the smile, but Alex could tell she still smiled because of two dimples in her cheek. He felt the desire to brush his fingers lightly across the cheek and then trace the jawline back to the firm chin and touch her lips. *How exotic she is.* His breath came faster. *Her jaw shouldn't be so long.* Alex froze and then took a quick step back.

The girl dropped her hands and turned a pleading face toward him. *Her eyes are too big to be normal.* She lifted her hands and the robe slipped over her skin to show long graceful arms. "Don't be afraid. I love you." She paused, mouth slightly open, and Alex could see her sharp pointed teeth. *She's an alien.* He tried to scream, but nothing would come out. He tried to turn and run, except he had lost all control of his body. He grew more and more terrified as he watched her come closer. She lifted one hand to the side of his face and then he felt it playing in his hair. In a sultry voice she whispered in his ear. "It won't hurt you, too much."

She slipped back and he watched her lips pucker for a kiss and felt his own responding for the contact. *I want to kiss her.* Then he was awake and gasping in the holo-field. "No. No. No. Gross. I do not want to kiss an alien."

~**********~

A teenage girl, almost a woman, hurried through the corridors. She had delicate features, with large violet eyes, and the top of her pointed ears stuck up out of her shoulder length, white hair. When she saw her father ahead of her, she slowed to his pace. He stopped at the door to the Weird room and she stopped. Then, hesitantly she approached, remembering what was hanging in her room's closet and the note her father had left for her. It had read, "Hheilea, this is your time. You need to begin preparations. Amable has given me permission to use the Weird room. Meet me there."

Her father turned toward her, not looking directly at her. She heard her father answer her future question, "I cannot tell you who it will be. The *t'wasn't-to-be-is* ceremony will give you that answer."

Hheilea stood still gritting her teeth. *I hate being a kimley. I have to pretend to be a boy and look like a kid, instead of young woman. No one else can ever understand how terrible my life is. My father can't see me smile at him. Instead he sees the future. He tries to talk to me, but he's talking to my possible future. His subconsciousness lives in 'now', but what good does that do me?* Hheilea looked at her father, her mouth firmly shut refusing to ask the question he had already answered even as she heard it in her mind. *Who will he be?* Her older cousin had been the only possibility she knew of, but he'd been kidnapped.

Sweat stood out on her father's forehead. "For your sake and the sake of what's coming, I'm trying to get as close to 'now' as I can."

Excitement tried to bubble up in her, but her fear tamped it down, even as she thought the *t'wasn't-to-be-is* must be drawing her future husband toward her. A young kimley man must be traveling to the academy or might be there already. *What would her future husband look like?* Her father's difficulty spoke of why she didn't want to be an adult. Once she matured, she would never live again in 'now' like all other creatures. *I'll be another oddity, just someone to kidnap and torture in order to get answers about the future.* She didn't want to live in the future like her parents. Again her father spoke. "I'll wait for you inside." And then he entered the doorway.

He knows I don't want to do this and will put off entering the Weird room. Fighting against her fears and wanting to go against the future he saw, she rushed through the door after him. Her emotions shook her body as they stood in a featureless, white room.

Her father turned around to face her and the doorway. He

wasn't quite looking at her. A grin covered his face. "The future probability showed you not coming in for a long time, but knowing my daughter's strength of will, I suspect you fought your natural inclination and came in right behind me. I also expect you to be pretty upset. I was too, at this time of my life. We've come to the Weird room, because of what you're going to do. The Weird is a secure place for your subconsciousness to take care of your body for the first time."

Hheilea wanted to grin back, and she wanted to slug him. Tears of frustration rolled down her checks, and she swung at him, knowing his subconscious would see and block the blows. Briefly, they sparred, until she stopped gasping for breath.

Her father held out a hand with a vial. "Take this, drink it, and hold my hands."

Hheilea stood for a long time looking at the vial. *What is it? Is this the beginning of the end of being conscious of my surroundings?* Finally, she opened the vial, and drank it all in one gulp. The liquid burned down her throat, leaving her gasping. Hheilea desperately lunged for his hands, as vertigo temporarily made her dizzy. The room around her faded away, leaving Hheilea standing with her father on gray, gently, shifting ground. Around them were colors like shifting panes of colored glass hanging in the air. She started to drop to the ground, overwhelmed by the experience, but strong arms caught her, holding her up. "Oh my daughter, how I have looked forward to this."

Those words didn't sound right to Hheilea. *It sounds as if he's in the 'now' or maybe, and she gulped at the thought, I'm in the future with him.* She looked up to gaze into his eyes, and he winked at her and said, "Come on, our family's anxious to see you."

He reached toward a green pane, and his hand disappeared into the color, followed by the arm, and then his body streamed into and was absorbed by the green.

Eyes wide in wonder, Hheilea's hand held by her father, and then her whole body entered the color after him. Green surrounded her, and she stood in a different place, and a group of people crowded forward. Hheilea backed into her father and gasped. She recognized her grandparents, but they were dead. *How could they be here? And who were all of the others?*

Her dad said, "Everyone, here's Hheilea."

She stepped forward and hugged her grandparents, long separated from her, but confusion made her stop, pull back, and look around. "How are you all here?

Many different voices spoke at once. One of the ladies she didn't recognize shouted, "Quiet!" She continued in a lower volume. "Hello, dear. I'm you great-great-great-grandma. In your bewilderment, you've forgotten your lessons. Our consciousness lives in the future and travels through time. Remember, dear, for us time isn't a dimension as most creatures treat it. Time itself has dimensions. We're all in time. I came from your past to this location in time to see you."

Another lady came up to her. "The last time I held you was when you were just a little baby. Let me hold you."

Hheilea held both hands up to ward off the stranger and stepped back. Her eyes filled, and tears threatened to fall. She remembered the lessons taught at home in the dining room. Anger and frustration pushed away the perplexity. Questions bubbled up in her. Her voice cracking with emotion, she asked, pleading for an answer, "Why? Why if we are so powerful? We can see into the future and travel through time. Why have we let our people get captured and sold into slavery?"

Everyone stepped aside, and an old man stepped forward. "Hello, Hheilea. Small things are easy to avoid, but each choice makes a new future. There is one big danger looming in the future with only one possible way to defeat it. We choose the path of hope for everyone's future. You may have heard the saying 'With great power comes great responsibility.' It also comes with many painful choices."

Her father nodded at the words, "Her time with us is up. I must take her back to her body. Goodbye. Come with me Hheilea."

Taking her hand, he reached for a red pane. With her free hand, she waved goodbye to all the family members, and then red surrounded her. Again, she stood alone with her father back on the first, gray landscape and she asked, "What did the old man mean?"

Her father looked at her. "Being able to see possible futures doesn't make us all powerful. Sometimes pain and suffering are the only way to get to the best future and we have to make a difficult choice." And then he hugged her.

Again, the tears flowed. "Why haven't you done this before, Daddy?"

He sighed as he looked back at her. "The potion in the vial only works when you're beginning into the t'wasn't-to-be-is. Your subconscious has noticed the beginning changes for your t'wasn't-to-be-is ceremony. But you'll still be confused and puzzled until the ceremony begins in earnest. All children get this experience at your age. Soon you'll no longer be a child. This experience showed you what it's like to be an adult kimley and will encourage you not to fight against the changes happening to you. When the moment is right, you'll know your time as a child is at an end. When that time comes to pass, the t'wasn't-to-be-is plant will bear fruit, and you'll begin the dance to become one with your life's partner.

"Your time here is done. You're returning to 'now.' I love you."

Then they were back in the Weird room, and her father wasn't quite looking at her.

Chapter Five
Hheilea

In the morning, Hheilea and her brother, Hymeron, ran through the passageways. Hymeron, a good eight inches shorter than Hheilea, was obviously younger. They both wore baggy, gray pantaloons with colorful vests.

Hymeron laughed and said, "I'm looking forward to having him in our control. Remember you agreed to do what I want."

Hheilea didn't say anything. Troubled thoughts bothered her as they drew near to the clinic. *This human had been part of why Mom's sick. It was Mom's choice, but this human's existence caused the problem.* She nodded and said, "Yes, he's going to pay."

Light-footed, they dodged around other aliens in the passageways. Hheilea slowed as they came near the clinic. Hymeron snickered.

Stick, with a holographic display of pictures and text surrounding him, entered the clinic ahead of them. The holograph itself was transparent. As he walked, he waved his hands through the air. In response, the information around him changed, and one picture brought a chuckle from him.

Hymeron gave a hand signal to Hheilea. Meanwhile, voices came from the clinic. Ignoring the voices, the two of them snuck into the room behind Stick and tripped him. Immediately, they ran back into the passageway, laughing quietly. Behind them, Hheilea heard the crash of the man falling, followed by someone laughing.

Stick wailed. "No!"

Hheilea came to a stop with her brother. Remorse

extinguished her laughter. The next moment, a hand grasped her shoulder, and she saw Hymeron caught by another hand. Amable frowned at them and dragged them into the clinic. "Are you all right, Stick?"

In the clinic, Alex and Gursha finished helping Stick to his feet. At first, Stick didn't answer. He let Gursha hold his face against hers as she whispered to him, and then pushed away from her to face Amable, "No. I'm not all right. I just lost months of paperwork, thanks to those two troublemakers."

"Months?" Amable asked, raising a single bushy eyebrow.

"Okay, days," Stick said. "But still, I thought you were going to do something about them terrorizing me."

"I'm giving Hhy and Hymeron a job right now. Also, if I hear of them causing more problems, they will be confined to their quarters."

"Great, just great. If Alex's training must go forward, then I'll take my contrary opinion to tech support and try to get my files recovered."

Amable said, "Go ahead and good luck."

Before Stick left, Alex spoke up. "Your nose—it's blue."

"Of course, it's blue," sputtered Stick. "Whenever it gets hurt, it turns blue. That's normal."

Amable looked down at Hheilea and Hymeron. "This is Alex. Remember what I told you about behaving." Then Amable looked back up and said to Alex, "Hhy and Hymeron are your trainers."

Alex looked after the departing Stick, not paying attention.

"Alex, did you hear me?" Amable asked. "These two boys, Hhy and Hymeron, are going to give you training and exercise."

"What?! Alex stepped back, accidently activating a holo-field. Alex screamed as he was lifted up into the air and the two kimleys laughed as Alex waved his arms and legs about in a comical struggle. He cut the scream off and glared at them. Breathing deep he turned a pleading look at Amable. "I'm still trying to get used to being in an alien place, with strange creatures, and you're going to stick me with them?"

"Yes, Hymeron and Hhy Soaley. They're brothers."

Hheilea grinned at his consternation, not noticing the quiet notes of a song in her head. *Life would be so much easier if I didn't have to hide and act like a boy. And I don't like being called Hhy.*

Her brother said, "You're funny. Could you wave your arms and legs about again?"

Sounding desperate, Alex said, "But they're just little kids."

Hheilea stood up straight and stomped up to Alex, tipping her head to look him in the eyes as she did. The top of her head came up just short of Alex's chin. "I'm not that much shorter than you, you big lump, so don't call me a little kid."

"Have fun. I'll see you later." Amable's ear tufts gently waving, he made his escape from the room.

"Wait! Come back! Don't leave me with them."

Hymeron laughed and said, "If you're done eating, let's go."

Alex checked his shoes before looking at the kimleys. Hheilea looked back at him. *I wonder how old he is. He's the kid, not me.*

Alex opened his mouth, hesitated, and asked, "Where are we going?"

"To give you some exercise," Hheilea said. She ignored the distant sounds of music in her head and walked away with a laugh.

As Hheilea walked with them down the hall, she thought back to her experience with her dad. Vaguely, she heard Hymeron talking to Alex.

Then Alex screamed, "Aaah!"

Hheilea stopped and looked back. Alex stood looking down a passageway, talking to himself.

"A huge spider, I'm going to be frightened. I don't want to be frightened. Wait, I'm not really frightened, just a bit scared." Alex continued talking to himself, but too quietly for her to hear.

This human boy's crazy. She turned to her brother to see what he thought. Her brother had a most disappointed look on his face.

Hymeron told her. "Earlier, Gursha told me via my AI, she

would give him a drug forcing him to face his fears and analyze how he felt. I thought he would be crying and screaming for help."

His expression changed to a hopeful look and he added. "At least the special experience I've prepared should be fun."

When Hymeron stopped she did too. The second time Hymeron stopped, she waited trying not to think about what Hymeron was doing to the human. A flowery fragrance caught her attention. *Is there a winkle around?* A quiet voice made her look back at the human. Alex stood, lips puckered, and a winkle girl leaned seductively against him. Hheilea gasped, feeling warmth in her cheeks. A thought blazed across her mind. *What's that minx doing? She better not....* Hheilea turned on her brother and slugged him. "What are you doing working with a winkle? You know how cruel they are."

Hymeron stepped away from her. "Get a grip on yourself. I'm just having some fun."

Hheilea warred with the ideas of strangling her brother or running over to tackle the winkle. At a gasp of pain from Alex, Hheilea whirled around. The human stood against the wall blood dripping from his chin. *My brother's gone too far. This is wrong.* A young lepercaul thundered down the hall and attacked Alex. Hheilea lost all restraint. Her brother grabbed her as she growled and started to go to Alex's aid. She didn't have any plans for what to do against the eight foot tall and four foot wide creature. She wasn't thinking, just reacting. Hheilea fought him, until help in the form of Alex's flock leader showed up.

Ytell hollered from the other end of the hall. "Enough! Leave my flock member alone!"

The winkle and the lepercaul ran back through the doorway they had come from. Ytell ruffled his feathers and in a very upset tone said, "Hymeron, you do not want to be in trouble with me. Take Alex to the Weird room. Now."

Her brother spoke in the petulant tone she hated. "Okay don't get your feathers all fluffed up. I was going to stop it before they hurt him, much. Come on, Alex."

In a quieter voice he added to Hheilea. "I wasn't letting them hurt Alex, just roughing him up a bit. It's good training for him. He needed to see the reality of his situation. You and I know this is a dangerous situation for everyone, but Alex didn't. Now he does."

Behind them Alex walked at an increasingly slower pace. Then he spoke with anger in his voice. "Isn't that the same door we went past earlier? At this rate, when I arrive at wherever you're dragging me, I'll be too tired to exercise."

"It's only been about thirty minutes," Hheilea answered. "Although he's right we should stop going in circles and get him to the Weird room."

Hymeron looked at both of them. "Oka—"

The door opened and a familiar translucent head looked out into the hall. The creature spoke interrupting Hymeron. "Hi. Humans do taste good."

Hymeron said, "Where's Twarbie? She was supposed to take you back to your wild space."

The baby laughed. "I told her to take me back. She leaned against the wall and said, 'I like that boy.' Then, I thought about human. I wanted to eat him."

Everyone stood still for a second and then Hymeron said, "Your job's over and you're supposed to return to your wild space."

"Don't want to." Whined the baby lepercaul and then in a deeper confident tone said, "I'm going to eat human."

Hymeron retreated a step. Blusteringly he said, "You can't do that."

Hheilea considered the conversation even as she whispered to Alex. "Start walking away." *Why do I have a brother? Boys are such a pain. The winkle likes Alex? I don't believe it.* Hheilea stepped toward the baby even as Hymeron backed up. In a calm voice, she said, "If you try to eat the human, your parents will be mad at you and take away your favorite foods."

The baby reached a giant hand toward Hheilea and she flinched but stood still. "You don't—"

The baby spoke over her voice. "Parents don't care about others. How do you taste?"

The lepercaul lunged at Hheilea in a surprisingly fast move for the creature, but she ducked. The lepercaul's arm swung into and slipped past her head. Burning pain ripped across her skull and white hair drifted toward the floor. The floor seemed to rise to meet her, but she twisted and caught herself with one hand. Spinning she slammed the other hand down. She looked up from her awkward position to see the baby laugh at her as he swiped at her midriff with a massive hand. Hheilea dropped to her back and rolled. All the time she expected to feel pain explode as the blow connected, pinning her to the floor. Instead there was just a tug on her vest. A trickle of pain down her back accompanied the tug on her clothes. Frantic, Hheilea continued the roll back to her feet. She thrust against the ground and sprinted, screaming, "Run!"

Alex responded to her command by shutting his mouth and turning to run away. Hymeron sprinted past Alex. "Follow me. He can't run as fast as us and we'll get away."

Hheilea ignored her vest flapping loose on her arms. However, she couldn't ignore the unfamiliar freedom from the binding. Her chest bobbed and swung with each step she took. Anger and pain filled her voice as she yelled at Hymeron. "Call Ytell about the wild baby."

Hymeron yelled back. "I got ahold of Twarbie, the winkle. She's supposed to return the baby to its wild."

Too quickly Hheilea caught up with Alex. *If we survive, I'm going to strangle my brother. This human better not see* ... She held an arm against her chest. Behind her, the thudding of the baby's running interrupted her thoughts. "Can't you go faster?" She half asked and half demanded of Alex.

Alex shook his head and gasped. "No... too... tired."

Hheilea wanted to scream. She moved up beside him and shouted at Hymeron. "We need another plan! The baby's going to catch us!"

The human said, "Leave..."

"Go faster," Hymeron shouted back.

"me.."

"Alex can't!"

"behind."

"I'll open a Utility portal!"

A swirling pattern formed quickly on the wall, widening to reveal a large hole. Hymeron dove through it. "Hurry up," he called out to Alex and Hhy. "Hopefully he's too big to follow us."

The thumping footsteps drew nearer every second. Fear and the memory of the pain from the lepercaul pushed Hheilea to go faster. Instead, she slipped an arm behind Alex and gripped the top of his pantaloons. She dove, jerking him after her. Her arm twisted and she felt her hand slip loose. *Will he make it?* She was through the hole and tumbling. The weight of another body slammed into her. Together they tumbled to a stop with Alex pinning her, face down. "Get off me, you big lump."

Then she felt his hand on her back shoving her harder into the floor. "Hey!"

Hymeron said, "Hurry up, you two. The baby's trying to get through the hole."

The weight shifted. Bitterly she thought. *At least I'm on my stomach. I'm so looking forward to being done with this human.* She scrambled up to her knees and crawled away from the hole. Her blouse hung loose in front of her. *Great. Just great. Why don't I just rip it all the way off and make sure everyone finds out I'm a girl. Then I can stop hiding and face my doom.*

Voices spoke in the dim light

"Hey, watch where you're going."

"What are you doing in here?"

Snakelike creatures slithered on the floor.

Alex gasped out an apology. "Sorry.... The back... of your clothes... are ripped... and I think you're bleeding."

Standing up Hheilea looked back. She saw Alex against the light from the hole. *Good thing guys are so dumb or he might notice I'm a girl.* Furiously she said, "Don't look at me. Keep moving. It can reach through the hole. You're too close to the opening."

Clenching her teeth she tucked her blouse into her pantaloons.

A big thump, followed by a whining voice signaled the baby's attempt to get through the portal. "Stop running. I'm hungry." A pause and they heard, "Oh. I could eat these things."

Alex stopped to look back. "What are they?"

Flashes of light from behind them lit up the dim passageway. *I doubt the baby will like getting shocked.* Hheilea caught up to him, tugged on his arm. "Come on we've got to keep going. The Zorms won't distract it for long. They're more mechanical than flesh and won't let the baby eat them. They've been exploring the ship since the slaves rebelled against the ship's original owners, the Deems. They also help with the ship's maintenance."

Movement to the side caught her vision. *Reflections.* Crystals leaned against the wall. Sounds of the fight faded as they moved on.

Hheilea said, "Be careful. We don't want to break these crystals. Deems are the only ones who know how to grow some of them."

Both of them slowed. A colorful, pulsating glow came from around a corner. They walked around the bend and stopped. Alex gazed in wonder. Instead of a passageway there was a crystal forest. Each crystal pulsed and coruscated with different colors. Hymeron waved. "Come on."

Carefully they walked into the forest. More of the snakes slithered about. Alex reached out to touch a crystal and Hheilea slapped his hand away. "Don't touch them."

Alex said, "They look alive."

Hymeron said, "They are. We're in a secret garden. I've helped the Zorms procure some things for their experiments. So they're okay with us being here, but don't tell anyone else about this. They hold grudges and you don't want to find out how they get even. If we damage these crystals I'd either do what they said or suffer the consequences."

Hheilea said, "Uh, oh."

A familiar thumping sound grew louder. Hheilea grabbed Alex by the hand again. "Run."

Hymeron shouted. "Come on you two! We've got to get out of here!"

Hheilea wrapped a strong arm around Alex's back and supported him as they continued on. "It's no use. We can't outrun it. This time you've really gotten us into bad trouble, Hymeron. You need to call Ytell or Amable for help."

"No, we can't call them from here." Hymeron's words snapped out of him. "This'll work. When this portal opens get through it quickly. It won't stay open long. So don't wait or you could get stuck in it. Just don't break any crystals."

A shimmering in the air caught Hheilea's attention. In a second the shimmering spread in a circle, leaving a view of the normal hall in the middle.

"Jump!"

Hheilea jumped, pulling at Alex as she went and then she was tumbling on the passageway floor. *What was that snapping sound?* This time she shoved away from Alex trying to keep her clothing covering her front. She didn't wait for him or help him, but leapt to her feet. Hymeron already stood by the Weird room door and she moved to join him.

From behind her she heard Alex ask, "Where's the baby?"

Hymeron said, "The baby? You mean the terror. If it didn't break any crystals, then Twarbie will find it and get it back to its wild. If not... well... the Zorms will take care of it."

Hheilea opened the door and entered. The room was empty and completely white. She remembered her brother's plans and slumped against the wall. *I don't like this.* "Hymeron, use your AI to talk to the Weird about healing my AI and me. Also I need some new clothes."

Immediately her ripped blouse was gone replace by a new one and the familiar binding of a vest. "Never mind," she said. "The Weird room heard me without my AI working."

Hymeron said to Alex, "If you have any energy left, start your training."

Alex looked around. "Uh, there's nothing in here."

Hymeron pointed at Alex. "Start running, unless you're wimped out."

"Where to?"

"That wall."

"Ha. The wall. Right." Alex took a couple of strides but didn't reach the wall. Hheilea watched Alex's expression and laughed at his surprise.

"What's going on?" Alex asked in amazement as he started to run.

Alex stopped after half-a-dozen seconds. With his hands on his knees, he asked between pants, "Why do I ... never get ... closer ... to the wall?"

"This is a special place in many ways," Hymeron said. "It's called the Weird. The Weird isn't the name of this room as much as it is the artificial intelligence running this room. You're going to stay in this room until your training is done. It'll provide everything you need until you leave. Look at what it did for us."

Hheilea relaxed in a chair, holding a tall, cold drink. She could see a little bit of the holo-field the Weird had around her head as it healed her AI. The feeling of her hair growing back made her want to find a mirror. A variety of snacks covered a small table between her and where Hymeron rested in a chair.

Alex turned around and stared, open-mouthed, at them. "Where did all of that come from?"

"The same place as that chair," Hymeron said, snickering at the expression of surprise on Alex's face, as another chair appeared beside theirs.

"Actually, sweaty as you are, I bet instead of a chair, you'd enjoy a shower," Hheilea said, grinning. Having the Weird do things to this unsuspecting boy was fun.

"That would feel good. Where is it?" Alex looked around and then said to Hheilea. "What are you grinning about?"

Hheilea almost laughed out loud as the first drop of water hit Alex, who looked up at a small, dark cloud. Rain poured down onto the boy's upturned face. Stumbling, Alex tried to get away, but it followed him. Then he headed toward Hheilea with a determined look, and her eyes grew wide as she realized his plan. She quickly asked the Weird to stop the rain.

"Great, guys. Now how about some dry clothes?" Alex asked, laughing.

Giggling, they pointed to a new door. Alex cautiously approached the door. He returned in moments, wearing dry clothes.

After lunch and a nap for Alex, Hheilea and Hymeron took turns setting Alex up for pranks. She liked how easy going he was and tried to make her pranks something he might laugh at, but Hymeron took enjoyment in increasingly mean tricks. Last was another run at the wall, except this time, Alex ran into the wall and crumpled onto the floor, moaning in pain.

Hheilea stood and started to go to Alex, but Hymeron caught her by the arm and whispered fiercely at her. "Don't interfere. You promised to do what I want."

Hheilea glared at him and jerked her arm free.

Alex interrupted their argument by getting slowly to his feet. Panting and in obvious pain, he spoke in an accusatory tone. "You guys knew that was going to happen. I've had it."

Panting and weaving, Alex chased the kids until the floor turned slippery, his feet went out from under him, and he crashed limply onto the floor. A large, soft pillow appeared under his head just before he landed. In a second, he had fallen asleep.

Immediately, Hheilea turned and stormed across the floor at Hymeron. She jabbed a finger at him as he backed up until he fell. She spoke quietly but fiercely, not wanting to wake Alex. "You're being cruel. Sure, we're both upset about most of our people being slaves, but it really isn't everyone's fault. Amable, and all the others we live with are trying to keep us safe. In the past it felt good to do pranks, but at some point we have to grow up."

Hymeron said, "But he's the cause of Mom getting sick."

Hheilea swung her arm to point back at Alex. "This boy had nothing to do with Mom's decision."

Her ferocity shut up Hymeron. Immediately after saying, 'Mom's decision', Hheilea remembered the words of the old kimley man, 'You may have heard the saying with great power comes great responsibility. It also comes with many painful choices.' She said, "I was with Mom. Her cadley told Amable's team where to look for Alex. Mom knew the cost. Her act must have been important." And as she spoke, her own symbiotic cadley, a little green lizardlike creature with large, bright eyes, peeked out of her hair.

"It isn't fair that Mom's sick," Hymeron said.

Hheilea scowled. The fact that sharing information about the future can make an adult kimley sick irritated her and scared her, which irritated her more. "Of course, it isn't fair. Life isn't fair, but that doesn't mean we have to be horrible. Let's talk to him."

After a long pause, Hymeron said, "Ok."

She turned from her brother and headed for a door. "The Weird will let us know when he's waking up."

The door led to another area still within the Weird where they had everything they would need for the next months of the training. Hheilea was surprised at how much time passed before the Weird informed her Alex was waking up. *We really worked him too hard.* Walking toward Alex she smelled a strange flowery scent. "What's that scent?"

Hymeron asked, "What scent?"

It was gone. Hheilea wasn't sure if she'd imagined it. *For a moment I thought a winkle was here.* Using her AI she sent a question to the Weird. |Weird, where did the flower scent come from?|

She heard the response in her head. |Flower scent? What flowery scent? Maybe Alex knows.|

Hheilea snorted to herself. *The human's clueless about what's going on. It must be a strange joke the Weird's playing. I'll ignore it.* She said to Hymeron, "Remember what I said. We're going to treat him better."

Hymeron said, "I wasn't that hard on him. I still think you're over reacting because you're a g—."

"Hush," Hheilea hissed. "He might be awake."

Walking back to Alex, they stopped talking as she nudged him. "Alex, wake up."

"What?" Alex asked, rolling over.

"We'll have a snack and talk about your training," she said.

Alex said, "I'm too sore to eat."

"Okay," Hheilea said and had the Weird increase the smell of the food.

Alex sat up. "What are you guys eating?"

"Here's a bowl for you," Hymeron said.

Alex eagerly reached for the bowl and then paused, looking intently into Hymeron's face, "Is it safe for me to eat?"

Hheilea snatched the bowl from Hymeron and grasped a spoon that materialized in midair. She stirred the contents of the bowl and then took a bite. After swallowing, she said, "It's a little spicy, but safe."

Finally, Alex took the offered food, shoveled some into his mouth, and mumbled his thanks. Hheilea looked at the bruises forming on Alex's face. Even though they had been caused by her brother's pranks, she felt responsible. "How's your face?"

"Sore." Alex said, and after he swallowed, he continued. "What's with you two? Do you have to do so many stupid things?"

In a petulant voice, Hymeron said, "But we didn't do hardly anything."

Alex glared back. "The small rainstorm was kind of funny.

Making small, round rocks fly at me hurt. The pit that opened up in the floor scraped my legs pretty bad." Pointing at his bruised face and cuts on his arm, Alex added, "That doesn't cover the crazy time I had just getting to this room. I can go on."

"I thought it was funny," Hymeron said.

Alex pointed at his bruises and cuts. "Look at my face. Does that look funny?"

Hymeron glared back at Alex and then looked down at the floor. When Alex turned to glare at Hheilea, the tinkling notes of a wind chime softly played in her head, growing stronger. Hheilea still refused to acknowledge the music. "I'm sorry I got a little carried away with some of the pranks. I never wanted you to get hurt, but you can't understand what it's like being a kimley."

"A little?" Alex asked with a bitter laugh. "I don't care about your problems. They still don't give you an excuse to torture me or mistreat others."

"We—I didn't mean to hurt you," Hheilea said. "The Weird has controls to prevent anyone from dying, and it can heal you. I'm surprised it didn't heal you already. Maybe it wanted to keep the evidence."

"Why are you caving in?" Hymeron asked Hheilea. And then looking at Alex, he added. "And why do you have to be such a good sport about Hhy's pranks? You actually laughed at some of the things he did."

Red-faced, Hymeron stepped closer to Alex. "Hhy's behaving like a wimp, and I'm not surprised. Hhy's—." He stopped speaking and ground his teeth.

Alex shoved his face close to Hymeron's. "Hhy's what?"

Hheilea jabbed her brother in the ribs. *The idiot, he almost told my secret.*

Hymeron clutched his side and looked at Hheilea. "I'm sorry. The worst of what happened was my fault."

Alex stared at the two of them. "Okay, but do you two remember Amable's threat of confining you to quarters? If you go back to doing stupid pranks, Amable will hear about it."

"That's fair," Hheilea said. She turned away from them and spoke over her shoulder. "Race you to the top of the hill."

"What hill?" Alex asked.

Hheilea laughed, as a warm breeze brought the smell of salt water to her, and grass waved on the slope of a hill in front of them. Warmth on her skin made her look up. Instead of a ceiling, a violet sky with puffy, white clouds and two suns, one dull-red and the other yellow, met her eyes. From the bottom of the hill, she heard Alex ask, "What happened? Where are we?"

Hymeron said, "This is still the same room. Don't ask us how the Weird does this. We don't have a clue."

From the top of the hill, Hheilea watched Alex collapse on the ground from the effort of keeping up with her brother. *He doesn't know how to give up. If Hymeron will behave, I think we can have fun.* She still ignored the music, which, like the sound of approaching waves, grew in volume as she watched Alex.

Chapter Six
Practice

One evening, weeks later, the two suns had set, and clusters of bright stars started appearing in the sky. Hheilea sat by a fire, picking at her dinner. |*Weird, get us out of here.*|

Alex interrupted her attempt at getting the Weird to change the scene. "Wow, what a sunset or was it a suns-set?"

Hheilea quietly said, "This is the view from our home planet."

"Hhy, I bet you love it there," Alex said. Hheilea didn't say anything. "What's wrong?"

Hheilea frowned at him. *I don't want to be here ... It hurts to be reminded ..., and I don't want you learning about this ... You'll pity me.* "You aren't pronouncing my name right. It's Hhy, not Hi."

"I'm sorry, Hhhhy." Alex said and then reached toward Hheilea. "Why the sad face?"

Hheilea watched his hand moving toward her. *Please comfort me, and understand me.* Sighing, she said, "We've never been to our home world. No kimley lives there anymore. I wish we weren't reminded of it."

"What happened?"

Hheilea bit her lip. *Why does he have to keep asking questions? It hurts to talk about it. Can't he see my pain?* "Our people were attacked...and sold into slavery."

"That's terrible."

She shrugged. *It's worse than terrible.* "It isn't as bad now. Some of us have been freed."

Hheilea begged the Weird to change the scene and give them something to do. Then the stars were gone, and three game controllers appeared next to Hheilea. With a sigh of relief, she reached for one of them. "Now for some games."

"Wait," Alex said. "If your home world makes you sad, why did you have the Weird make it seem like we were on your home world?"

Hymeron scowled. "We didn't. The Weird decides the scenes. We can ask for things and make suggestions, but it's in control."

Surprised, Alex looked at Hheilea. She nodded in agreement. Alex said, "But, weren't you boys controlling my training?"

Hheilea stood up. *You're an idiot. Can't you see I'm not a boy? And I'm not a kid.* "We're just two kids good at playing pranks and games. The Weird doesn't need us for your training. Right now it looks like we should play some games."

"No, the Weird can wait," Alex said.

The ground shook, and a rumble filled the air. Hheilea thought to the Weird. *Thanks for having us play games.* With a relieved smile, she held a game controller out to Alex. "The Weird doesn't like to wait."

"Tough," Alex said. "I want to understand more about your past."

Hheilea dropped back to the ground and sat, head bowed, her white hair cascading over her face. Hymeron moved close to her and put an arm around her. "There isn't much to understand. We don't have any home world. Everyone uses or enslaves us. People kill us all the time, and there are fewer and fewer of us left."

Leaning forward, Alex placed a hand on Hheilea's shoulder. "That's terrible. Why are your people treated this way?"

Hymeron's mouth formed a straight angry line across his face. "You think *that's* terrible. Listen to this. It all started when other people in the galaxy found out about us. Our parents' conscious awareness lives in the future. That means they know some of the future possibilities. An adult kimley risks his health and life whenever he shares that knowledge with another individual. The more it affects the course of the present, the more likely the adult will die if he shares it. Others don't care about our lives. A few years ago, one individual killed thousands of kimleys, trying to learn more about the role of your planet in the future."

"Who?" Alex asked.

Hheilea jerked her head up to glare at Alex, and she spat the name. "Maleky."

"Most people are afraid to even say his name," Hymeron said. "Not us, we hate him. He kidnapped one of our cousins."

Alex's face registered his shock and he said, "At least you're safe."

Hheilea gave a short, bitter laugh. *I'll never be safe. And soon my life is going to change forever. I'm so frightened.* She said, "Our cousin was at the Academy when he was kidnapped, but we're not afraid."

Hymeron nodded. "He was almost as old as my sister, Hheilea, is now. That's the age we're in the most danger."

"I didn't know you two have a sister," Alex said.

Hheilea shrugged. "It doesn't matter. Someone will probably kidnap her or, if she's lucky, kill her in the attempt. No one cares enough to save m—, her."

Alex reached out to pull both of them into a hug and firmly said, "You said others don't care. Reconsider that statement. I care."

Hheilea held her arms crossed in front of her, as Alex hugged the two of them. *Why did I start to say me? He's going to find out I'm Hheilea. He's such an idiot. How can he not tell who I am?*

"Let's do the video games tomorrow evening," Hymeron said.

Alex said, "Good idea, Hymeron. Do you know the names of those spiral galaxies hanging above us?"

The night sky with stars had reappeared above them. Hheilea found the Weird had her lying in a hammock. Next to her, Alex and Hymeron each lay in separate hammocks suspended from trunks. High above them, feathery fronds moved against the night sky. In the background she could hear the lapping of waves.

~**********~

48

Hheilea woke, blinking in the bright morning light. She sniffed the air. *Argh, that smell. Every—* She ground her teeth in frustration. *And the Weird won't tell me what's going on. It's like it's teasing me with this flowery fragrance every morning. No use asking the Weird. It won't tell me. I might as well just ignore it.* Near her, but on small separate islands surrounded by water, she could see Alex and Hymeron sleeping in their hammocks. She grinned to herself. *Alex probably doesn't know the island he's on, is really a huge animal. Maybe I can get the Weird to surprise him.* Her hammock started to swing. Hheilea grasped the edges of her hammock and spoke to the Weird, |Weird, what are you doing?|

|I'm making your hammock swing.| Came the smug reply.

Hheilea knew the story about the Weird. How deems had one adversary whose wisdom had defeated their plans to destroy life in different solar systems again and again until finally, through overwhelming numbers, they were able to capture and kill him. Afterwords, out of respect and wanting to keep a great foe to practice against, the deems used a mind copy of the adversary to create the Weird. Hheilea asked, |Weird, why have you put us into a simulation of my people's home world? You're supposed to be so wise. Didn't you know how painful it would be?|

|Yes, I knew. I'm sorry for your pain.|

Hheilea asked, |Then wh—| Her hammock tipped, almost dumping her out, and Hheilea squealed. |Weird, stop it. You're going to dump me into the sea.|

|No, not the sea. I want you somewhere else.|

In the next instant, Hheilea was lying beside Alex, and he had an arm around her. The music in her head soared, and she rolled out of the hammock. Hheilea stumbled away quickly, her checks burning. Hheilea's quick exit swung the hammock, and dumped Alex and Hymeron, who had also been deposited into the hammock, onto the sand below.

Untangling himself from a struggling Hymeron and spitting out sand, Alex asked, "What happened?"

Hheilea said, "For some strange reason the Weird put me

in your hammock, and I jumped out."

Alex shrugged. "What? Why did you jump out?" Alex helped Hymeron to his feet, "Hhy, you're all red. Are you embarrassed? Why—? Oh, well I guess I don't know what's embarrassing for your people."

While Alex rambled, Hheilea went from embarrassed to furious. *Why can't he tell I'm almost a woman? I want to slap him.* She struggled to control herself. "I'm sorry. Being dumped into your hammock startled me."

Alex brushed himself off and awkwardly laughed. "Oh well, no harm done." Changing topics he asked, "Hhy? Something's been bothering me since last night. How come I haven't heard of your sister before?"

Hheilea froze. *What can I say?* She looked at her brother. They both turned to Alex and spoke at the same time.

Hheilea said, "She isn't on the ship."

Hymeron said, "She stays hidden in our rooms with Mom."

Alex asked, slowly puzzling things out, "Aren't your rooms on this ship?"

Again both kimleys answered at once.

Hymeron said, "I meant our rooms back at the Academy."

Hheilea said, "We aren't supposed to tell people she's on the ship."

Alex crossed his arms and frowning said, "You two are hiding something."

Again, the two kimleys looked at each other. Hymeron shrugged, and Hheilea turned to Alex. "I'm sorry, but for her safety, we don't talk about her."

In a rush and sounding a little desperate, Hymeron said, "Today we teach you how to play videogames, and Alex, you're so going to get beat."

Alex said. "Ha. You should know videogames are a teenage boy's favorite pastime on my world. You might not beat me as easily as you expect." In a more serious tone, he continued, "It's okay if you don't trust me with information about your sister, but please, don't lie. Everything's so strange. I don't know who to trust."

Hheilea hesitantly came up to Alex and gave him a hug.

"I'm sorry, Alex. I do want to trust you."

Hymeron spoke up louder than normal. "If you're good at videogames, the Weird will just make it harder all that much sooner."

Alex pushed Hheilea away forcing her to break the hug. He nervously cleared his throat. "Okay, Hymeron. Let's get started."

Hheilea nodded her head and swallowed as she looked back up at his intense blue eyes. She glanced over at Hymeron's worried expression and backed away from Alex.

~**********~

The next few days, they did exercise activities during the day, followed by videogames in the evening. One evening, Hymeron said, "You're doing great. I'm looking forward to tomorrow. We get to be in the game."

"What do you mean 'in the game'?" Alex asked.

"It'll be easier to show you," Hheilea said.

The next morning, the kimleys wore shorts and running shoes, with their white hair tied back in ponytails. Hymeron had ditched his shirt and vest, but Hheilea still had on a tight vest. In her hands she held a semi-translucent mass. "This is your new type of controller. It's a computer and much more."

Alex held up a hand and walked up to Hheilea. "Wait. I've wanted to ask why you're so different. Do kimley boys change as they get older?"

Hheilea's voice squeaked as she answered the question with a question. "What do you mean?"

Hymeron tried to interrupt. "We need to get going."

Alex moved closer to Hheilea. "Your voice is higher than Hymeron's, your legs are very slender compared to his, and your hips are wider. And your face is shaped much different. Like how I think an elven—."

Hymeron shoved between them. "Come on, we have to explain your new controller. Stop being goofy. Of course everyone's different."

Alex held his hands up in surrender. "Okay. How do I use this?"

Hheilea said, "Kneel in front of me."

When Alex knelt, she laid the mass on his head, and it flowed over his scalp. In a moment his hair poked through and his head looked normal except right at the edges. "It's your personal, artificial intelligence, AI for short. Stand-up and look at my scalp. Both Hymeron and I have one too. It interfaces with your brain. With your AI, you'll be able to communicate with other people and access other computers. Eventually, it'll develop its own personality." As she spoke, Alex looked down into her eyes. *Don't do that.* She turned her view to the ground and finished talking. "This AI will always be with you. Physically, I think you're doing great. Now we're going to help you learn things to survive out in the real world."

Hymeron impatiently said, "Let's get started. He'll catch on."

Suddenly, Hheilea stood with Alex and Hymeron on an eight-foot by eight-foot platform of grass. In front of it, other platforms, some short and some long, floated in the air. To the right and to the left, stone walls stretched forward out of sight. Alex moved to the edge of the platform and looked under it. Quickly, he backed up. "This platform is floating."

Hymeron shrugged. "Sort of. It's just like the first videogame we played, except now you're inside the game. The goal is to find the coins and exit to the next level without dying. After you finish this game, we're doing one where we can fight with swords. I'm looking forward to it."

"Without dying?" Alex asked, his voice squeaking. "I thought the Weird wouldn't kill anyone."

"You don't physically die," Hheilea said. "You won't feel pain if you miss a jump or get caught in a trap, like that one." She pointed toward a set of tall, sharp stakes standing in a pit. "You just lose a game life and then find yourself on a grass platform like this at the beginning of the level. If you lose too many lives, the game is over and you lose. I hope you beat this game quickly."

She watched the boys. Hymeron jumped to another platform, a wooden one, and Alex followed. A little later, Alex jumped at a moving grass platform, missed it, and let out a yell as he fell. Hheilea resolutely stopped watching Alex fall.

Falling doesn't really hurt. Beginning herself, she struggled to focus on her own progress.

Finally, Hheilea panting from the exertion, stood on the last platform. Only then did she give in to her desire to watch. After she waited for a long time, she caught sight of Hymeron. He jumped over a series of spinning rocks and dodged some swinging logs. Alex carefully mimicked Hymeron, following the path he took.

With one last jump the boys joined her on the platform. Immediately, all of them stood on a grassy hill. Above them, fireworks shot off. A victory song started playing.

Alex asked, "Now do we get to use swords?"

"You did a great job using your AI," Hheilea said.

"What?" Alex said. "I didn't need it."

"There's another game we could do. It would force you to use your AI more," Hymeron said with a grin.

Alex frowned. "You said we would do the sword fighting next." He paused and added, "but you said I would be learning things to help me survive in the real world. How will sword fighting help in the real world?"

Hymeron sat down. "The most dangerous threat in the universe is deems. Their technology is about the best in the universe. Most advanced weapons of your world will have limited use. But deems love physical fights and swords work great for fighting them, and for some deems, very special swords work the best."

"That's good to know," Alex said. "I remember Ytell talking about deems and they sound terrible."

Hymeron said, "They are. Did Ytell make clear that they aren't just beasts, but are actually very intelligent, with a higher level of technology than most other civilizations?"

"I think so," Alex said, and then he paused. "It's been a long time since I saw my friends in the flock. I want to get back. How fast can I do this sword training?"

Throughout this discussion, Hheilea didn't say anything. She didn't think they should move on. Alex's comment of not needing to use AI was bad. He needs to spend more time learning to use it. A realization reared up right after that. *I don't want Alex to go back to his flock. Being with him is fun.*

Hheilea's mouth dropped open at that thought, and then adamantly, she shook her head "no" to the thoughts. Hheilea told the Weird, |Take us to the sword training.|

The scene shifted, and everything changed. Hheilea stood on top of a stone tower, in the embrasure. A breeze played with her hair and flapped her long, loose, white dress. It took a second for the change to register, and then she became aware of something else. Music, haunting, mesmerizing music, played in her mind. The combination of having her secret identity exposed and acknowledging the music playing ripped a scream from her. "No!"

From below, Hymeron yelled, "Weird! What are you doing?"

Hheilea beat against the stone of the battlement with a fist, and again she screamed, "No!"

She heard Alex and looked down at him and her brother. "Hhy and your sister, Hheilea, are the same person."

Hymeron clutched his hair with both hands. "Yes. I don't know what the Weird's doing. It shouldn't have known about my sister. We've got to get her down. She needs to stay in her disguise."

Hheilea saw an arrow shoot into the ground at Alex's feet, and gave a gasp of fear for him.

Alex jumped back and shouted at Hymeron. "Someone's shooting at me! Why am I hearing music? And why do we need to get her down?"

"Hurry," Hymeron said, sounding desperate. "The Weird's starting this scene."

Another arrow struck near Alex's feet, and he dodged to the side. "Where are these arrows coming from? What am I supposed to do?"

Hymeron said, "The Weird's having the arrows fired at you. Use your AI. Just the same way you used it in the last game. That's how you made those jumps. Get your AI to use the closest gravity generators to lift you. That's the easiest way to go over the wall.

But he didn't use his AI, Hheilea thought. *I have to get the Weird to send us back to a practice scene where Alex can learn to use his AI.* But the Weird refused to respond.

Alex ducked behind a stump. "I don't understand. How can gravity lift me?"

Hymeron spoke quickly. "A gravity generator creates nuclei to pull you or an object toward them. Oh, and Alex, you might want to know you'll feel pain learning to sword fight."

Hheilea watched the scene below while trying to get the scene changed. Below her, Alex collapsed to his hands and knees. Frustrated and concerned, Hheilea stepped back from the battlement and looked for a trapdoor or some other way down. A scream interrupted her search. She raced back to the embrasure and anxiously scanned the area below. After a moment of searching, she spotted Hymeron gazing up into a tree. She gasped in alarm at seeing Alex's body hanging, jammed between two branches.

Hymeron called, "Are you okay?"

Alex moved, and she could hear his bitterness as he replied. "Fine, I'm just fine."

Giving up on finding a way down on her own, she continued to watch the events below. Slowly, Alex climbed down from the tree. He moved out into the open and suddenly, he rose straight up into the air, picking up speed as he shot above Hheilea. Up he went, growing smaller and smaller, and then he started coming back down. "Ahhhhhhh! Stop! Stop me!"

Chapter Seven
Sword Fighting

Hheilea found herself tied to a tree. A short, scruffy man holding a sword stood between her and Alex.

Alex collapsed on the grassy ground. "What happened?"

Hymeron said, "It took us out of that scene before you smashed into the ground and brought you here. You need to get it together."

Hheilea screamed. "Get back up! He's going to hit you with his sword!"

The fighter ran at Alex. "Eeyah!"

At the battle roar, Alex scrambled to his feet. Meanwhile, Hheilea frantically tugged at the ropes. She wanted to avert her eyes, but couldn't. Relief flooded her, as with a clang of steel meeting steel Alex blocked the attack. The next moment she screamed as he stumbled and the enemy's blade sliced toward Alex's throat.

The scene shifted, and Hheilea stood in a grassy dell with the boys and a tall man.

Alex asked, "What? What just happened?"

A blue and orange butterfly fluttered by Alex toward the tall man wearing a gray robe secured about the waist by a wide leather belt with a jewel-encrusted scabbard. It landed on the black pommel of the man's sword.

"He did a serviceable block," said the stranger, with a harsh voice, "but he needs practice on his footwork. Tripping during an attack is very dangerous. Of course, instead of trying the block, he should've moved in close and gutted his attacker."

"Who are you?" Alex asked.

"I'm Weldon, the legendary sword master," Weldon said, rubbing a scraggly brown beard with one hand as he looked Alex up and down. He turned and looked at Hheilea, giving her an abbreviated bow. "I didn't know we had a young kimley woman with us. Am I training this boy to help protect you? He isn't going to be proficient for a long time. I could come out and be your knight."

She flushed and opened her mouth to answer, but Hymeron interrupted. "Please keep it a secret. No one's supposed to know about my sister. She's been in disguise as a younger boy. I don't know how or why the Weird took her disguise away." He added to Alex, "Weldon's a computer character."

Again, Weldon stood still, stroking his chin, and absently spoke, looking off into the distance. "Hmmm. I'm going to have a chat with the Weird about this."

Annoyed and frustrated, Hheilea stomped forward, but her long, full dress snagged on a plant. She tugged it free. "Thank you for offering to protect me. I'll think about it."

Weldon said, "That dress isn't very practical for here. If the Weird insists on having you wear it, you could gird your loins."

"What?" she asked, perplexed.

Weldon removed his belt. With a series of movements, he gathered his robe until it was tied a knot in front of his waist. The robe still covered his torso, but from the waist down it looked like a bulky diaper. "I have done this before to get my robe out of the way. Now Alex, pull out your sword, and I'll start your training."

Following Weldon's example, Hheilea gathered the white dress up in front of her thighs, pulled it snug against her backside. A curt command came from Weldon. "Don't watch her."

Hheilea snorted and tucked the excess fabric between her legs and pulled it tight behind her. Gathering half of the material in each hand, she stretched the two ends around her hips and tied them into a knot. Without the dress to bother her, she stomped off into the bushes, and found a tree to sit against. Plopping down on the ground, she tried to ignore the sounds of the sword-fighting practice and her brother shouting words of either encouragement or derision. Closing her eyes, she considered the music she was hearing. Fear and uncertainty tugged at her. *It couldn't be the ... What else could it be?* She stayed there fighting with her own thoughts and ignoring the others' attempts to call her to lunch.

Eventually, the light of day grew dim until the dark shadows in the woods were broken only by the flickering fire in the clearing. Weldon and the boys called to her once again. The scent of hot food caused her stomach to growl in complaint of her fast. Alex's voice rose above the rest. "Come on, Hheilea. You have to be getting hungry."

Hymeron said, "When she's mad, it's best just to leave her alone. I'm going to get some more firewood."

Weldon said, "I'll help you."

Hheilea pushed herself up, and knocked the clinging leaves off her legs. She shoved her way through the bushes and stomped into the clearing. Alex stepped quickly toward her, and she turned away, but the fire blocked her escape. He touched her shoulder and said, "What's going on?"

She knocked his hand away. "Nothing's going on."

Alex said, "I understand you're upset, but ..."

Hheilea shoved at his chest, interrupting him. "You don't understand anything."

She followed up her first shove, intending to push him harder. The firelight lit up his eyes, and for a second, she gazed into them. Notes of music rose and fell, like the crashing of waves, and she shook.

Alex reached out and grasped her arms. "You hear this music too. What does it mean?"

"It doesn't mean anything!" she yelled at him, twisting out of his grasp.

At this point, Weldon strode into the clearing and tossed an armful of wood to the ground. He pulled his sword out and pointed to Hheilea. "Take that sword the Weird is offering you and try to hit me."

Hheilea snatched the sword hanging in the air and charged at Weldon, slashing at him from side to side. He backed up, just blocking her blows. They circled the fire, filling the air with the sound of ringing blows. Hymeron charged out of the woods and stopped to stand by Alex. They watched Hheilea slash at the tall man. Finally, Hheilea stopped, dropped her sword, and leaned on her knees, gasping for breath. Weldon slid his sword into its scabbard and untied a leather flask. He offered it to Hheilea. "Here, rinse out your mouth, spit, and take a sip."

Accepting the offer, she poured some of the cool liquid into her mouth, swished it around, and spit into the flames, where it sizzled. Lifting the flask again, she took a sip, swallowed, and then another. She handed it back to Weldon. "Thanks. I feel better now. Where's the food?"

Putting an arm around her shoulder, Weldon led her to the food.

~**********~

In the weeks following, Hheilea heard Alex try multiple times to talk to Hymeron about the music and ask about the danger she faced. Each time, Hymeron avoided the questions. She didn't want to talk with Alex about it either, except she had an annoying feeling she should be talking to him instead of just stealing glances at him. She hadn't paid any attention to the music, until the Weird forced her to wear a dress. *Alex is just my friend, just my friend..., just my—*. The memory of how it felt to be next to him in the hammock warmed her face, she ducked her head down, hoping no one saw her blush.

One warm afternoon smashing sounds echoed in the woods, as Alex defended himself from flying melons with a club. Hheilea leaned up against a tree with her head bowed, hair hanging over her face, and whittled while stealing glances at him. The discarded pieces of wood and occasional gasps of pain from nicking herself with the knife were testaments to how distracting she found him. Peeking at him increased the music which annoyed her, causing her to fiercely attack the piece of wood with her knife. The music would die down. She would sneak a look through her hair at him, and the cycle of music growing and her getting angry would start again. Eventually, Hheilea threw down the knife and her latest butchered piece of wood. She stormed off toward the woods, and Hymeron scrambled out of her way.

One step into the woods and the sound of smashing disappeared. Hheilea whirled about. The trees were gone, replaced by an open glade with flowering bushes, and a waterfall. Incensed at the change in scene, she yelled aloud at the Weird. "Oh, and now you'll change the scene for me. I told you Alex needs to go back and do some other games where he can learn easier." She tried again to communicate with the Weird through her AI. |What are you doing? He has to learn how to use his AI.|

She sat on the ground in surprise as the Weird answered for the first time since her disguise was taken away. |Hheilea, as a kimley, you have little reason to trust. But you—|

Hheilea wasn't about to listen to a lecture. She had questions. |Why don't you change the scene to where Alex can be taught to use his AI? Why do you insist on dressing me as a girl? How did you know I'm a girl?|

|Are you going to let me answer or just interrupt?|

She ground her teeth in frustration. |I'll listen.|

|As I was starting to say, you need to trust my plans. I—|

Hheilea jumped to her feet and shouted. "What do you mean, your plans? Alex needs to learn how to use his AI."

|Interrupt or listen?|

She flopped back to the ground and muttered, "Listen."

The Weird continued to speak in her head. |You and Alex have problems, but you need to understand about deems. They're the bigger issue. They created this ship, Weldon, and myself. You should never think of them as just beasts or monsters. They are very intelligent, and their technology in most ways is more advanced than other civilizations. They are the most pompous creatures I know of, and that can trick people into taking them too lightly. However, you can beat them. They aren't the smartest, wisest, or even the best fighters. Weldon was modeled on an amazing fighter who defeated deems again and again until they used superior forces to capture and kill him. I was modeled on another individual. Whoever it was out-thought deems a number of times, ruining their plans. I helped the slaves on board this ship overthrow the deems and capture this ship. Now I'm working on another way to thwart deems. Alex is important to this plan. You and Hymeron have done well with Alex, but he needs to be brought along just right. Be patient with me, or you'll distract Alex.|

|What are you working on that's so important?|

After a pause, she heard the Weird's answer. |Saving Earth.|

The glade disappeared and the sounds of fighting practice echoed through the forest. In a few steps Hheilea returned to the rest of the group. Alex stood knee-deep in the smashed remains of dozens of melons.

Weldon sat on a branch above everyone, and dropped one last melon at Alex. "That's enough strength training for today. Now we'll work with swords, but with something new added in. I'm happy with your progress. You're starting to anticipate my attacks. That's very important for any form of fighting. Remember to always watch your opponent's eyes. This will help you prepare for their attack. I haven't figured out why your ability to anticipate an attack is worse at times. For example, you weren't doing very good anticipating melons during the last twenty minutes, but the last few times you did great. Also, you need to be quicker with the tierce block. We'll work on it today. I don't know what your schedule is like, but when you have time, make sure you come back. Have your AI bring up Weldon, the Sword Master. In a year, I might be willing to admit I taught you."

"Okay," Alex gasped as he smashed the last melons flying at him from all directions. Covered in melon gore, he added, "Can I wipe my face off?"

"Better than wipe it off," Weldon gruffly said. "Just get rid of it, like this."

All of the melon gore disappeared from Alex, and where he had been wading in gore, he now stood balanced on a log.

"You could've done the same with your AI. It can communicate with the Weird." Weldon levitated into the sky. "Follow me."

Alex stood on the ground, looking up at Weldon. "I can't get up there."

"What?" Weldon shouted. His face turned a dark red, and his eyeballs bulged out. Swooping out of the sky, he shook a fist in Hymeron's face. "You've brought me a wet-behind-the-ears kid, who can't even use his AI! This is ridiculous. Come back when he's ready." Weldon vanished.

Alex threw his club down. "Doesn't he know the Weird is in control of my training? It isn't our fault."

"He'll get over it," Hymeron said.

Hheilea watched the boys in silence. Had she seen Weldon wink at her? The Weird had told her, he had a plan for Alex and it entailed bringing him along just right.

Alex glanced at Hheilea and turned away. "Is Weldon really just a computer character? He has such strong emotions. It's like he's real."

Hheilea didn't try to hide her exasperation. "Of course he's real. Don't you pay attention? Remember him eating fish with us around the fire?"

Alex held his hands up in puzzlement. "What? Either he's a computer character or real."

Hheilea forced herself to speak in a calmer voice. "Look, he's just another type of AI. Some people call them RE because they have a real existence. You need to talk more to your AI. It won't respond much at first, but it will react to simple requests, such as, 'find a local gravity generator and lift me.' You just need to learn how to define what you mean by 'lift me.' Your AI is a baby, and working with it can be interesting."

Hheilea remembered Alex's first attempts to use his AI and laughed before she continued. "Over time it will learn and as a result respond to you better. Also, it grows in abilities to fit who you are. I've heard of a few people who manage to develop incredible AI, but we haven't seen anyone do that."

Hymeron stood up. "You're going to play a new game. It's similar to the first game, but first, we should eat and you need rest."

Chapter Eight
The First Fight

In the new game, Hheilea stood on a grassy platform next to a pile of snow. Leaning down, she scooped up some snow and began to make a snowball. *Finally the stupid Weird put me back into pants.* She thought briefly of the dress hanging in her closet. *It would be fun to wear a dress like it.* She grinned, looked at Alex, and turned away. *If only the music would stop, I could have fun. I do like Alex, but he's a human and just a boy.* Around the three of them floated other platforms, in all directions. Scattered about the platforms were tubs of mud, buckets of water, and piles of snow. Hymeron and Alex stood on their own platforms. Green holograms with the number zero floated over both of their heads.

Hymeron tossed a snowball from hand to hand. He threw it, hitting Alex.

"Hey," Alex said.

"Look up," Hheilea said, pointing over Alex's head.

Above Alex flashed a slightly yellow, green hologram with the number one displayed.

"When that number reaches sixty, you lose. Dunking you in a tub of mud is thirty points," Hymeron said. "The color also changes from green to orange as you get hit. Good luck." Then both kimleys started belting Alex with snowballs.

He jumped toward another platform but missed and plummeted toward the ground. Hheilea stopped throwing snowballs and silently cheered Alex on. *Come on Alex you can do it. Get your AI to move you.* Just before Alex hit the ground, his body jerked up into the air. Hheilea grinned at the sight of Alex's success. He flew through the air and tried to land on a different platform, but he had too much forward momentum and tumbled off the far side of it. Hheilea picked up more snow and paused to watch Alex land face first on a lower grass platform.

Hymeron continued to fire snowballs as Alex's hologram turned orange with the numbers rapidly increasing. He said to Hheilea, "What's with you? Keep throwing."

~**********~

Two weeks later, still in the same scene, Alex jumped toward a platform. Hheilea fired snowballs at him, but his grass platform flipped up just in time. Alex said, "Hah—I blocked you this time."

"Look up," Hheilea said, laughing as she used her AI to dump snow onto Alex.

That evening, Hheilea and Hymeron sat beside Alex, holding sticks and roasting a marshmallow-type treat over a lava flow. A barren mountain rose into an orange sky. Out of the mountain top, a fountain of lava shot a thousand feet into the air. The crescent of a giant planet hung above them, filling most of the sky. Hheilea watched her treat slowly browning and said to Alex, "You're quiet tonight. Are you getting discouraged?"

"I just want to be done and get back to the flock. We've been in the Weird's world forever. I'm still puzzled about how it makes these worlds and I really don't understand what the Weird is. You've said it's a computer, but other times, it sounds like another AI.

A bubble in the lava popped, throwing tendrils of lava up into the air. Hheilea jerked her treat back. One of the tendrils hit Hymeron's marshmallow treat, melting into it, and in a second, flames covered the remains of the treat. Hymeron tossed the stick onto the lava, where it burst into flames. He held a hand out, and another stick with a marshmallow treat appeared. With a long sigh, Hymeron looked at Alex. "The Weird is another AI, and it's in a computer of its own. You're supposed to figure your AI out on your own, but you're taking forever. Your AI interfaces with other computers."

Alex said, "I'm trying, but you're making it too hard."

"I'm sorry. Don't give up. You're getting better," Hheilea said.

Hymeron poked his sister. "Stop being such a softy. He's pretending. Trying to get us to take it easier and give him a chance to beat us."

Hheilea looked at Alex just in time to catch him grinning, before he hid it with a pretend yawn. She gazed at him in surprise, and he shrugged and winked at her. *He made a fool of me on purpose.* Hheilea jumped to her feet and tossed her stick down. "Come on, Hymeron, let's go to our room and get some sleep."

"Okay. I'm coming. Just don't act so bossy." Hymeron pulled his sticky treat off the stick he held and popped it into his mouth.

The next day, Hheilea stood next to Hymeron on a platform. Again, they encouraged Alex to gain a better understanding of how to use his AI, even as they worked at beating him. Hheilea shouted at Alex, "You're moving much better through the air. I think you've made a breakthrough with your AI. Did you practice last night?"

Alex didn't answer, and she lost sight of him. "Where did Alex go?"

Hymeron shouted, "He's over here."

She saw Hymeron throwing snowballs at Alex, but he suddenly stopped and threw his hands up. "He's just standing there. What's he trying to do. We're going to be stuck in here forever."

Hheilea joined him. "No, Alex is up to something."

Hymeron said, "Are you—."

Alex disappeared. Hheilea gasped and looked around trying to spot him. "Where did he go?" Balls of sloppy mud started pummeling her.

"Over here!" Hymeron shouted, jumping onto a platform to escape the blizzard of mud. Hheilea jumped after him. Something shoved her, and she crashed into Hymeron.

"Aaahh! You're knocking me off." Hymeron slid toward the edge.

"No, the platform's tipping us off." With a splash she landed in cold, soupy mud with her brother.

"I hope I wasn't too rough on you little kids," Alex said from above them.

Covered in mud, Hheilea stood with her fists on her hips. "I'm not a little kid." And then she laughed. "You did it."

Alex stood looking back at her. His triumphant look faded, his face turned red, and he mumbled. "No, you're definitely not a little kid." Jumping off his platform, he flipped through the air. "I'm finally starting to enjoy this. You know, I've really gotten to like you two. This training has been fun, and I'm feeling much stronger. But I'd like to return to my flock."

"You're not done yet," Hymeron said. "The Weird says you need to go back to the castle and rescue the fair maiden." And then he grumbled discontentedly, "At least no RE that can leave the computer world has seen Hhy is actually Hheilea, except for Weldon. And he is the epitome of trust."

~**********~

Hheilea found herself back on the stone tower in a dress. Resignedly she looked down at it and then she smiled. *It's like the dress in my closet.* She pirouetted and sighed to herself. *If only there was a young kimley man here.* Frowning, she walked over to the crenelated, stone edge of the tower. Peering over the edge, she called out. "Alex, save me and we can get out of here."

Below, she saw Alex smoothly rise up from the ground into the air. Hheilea gasped at the sight of archers preparing to shoot Alex. She took a breath to scream a warning, but before she could, the archers were all wrapped up in ropes. Relaxing, she grinned in relief. *He's doing great. We'll be out of here soon.* Alex continued through the air toward her and then slammed to a stop. She almost laughed aloud at the sight of his face smashed against an invisible wall, but a guttural cry from below drew her eyes down. At first she couldn't see anything, but the voice sent a chill down her spine.

"Are you ready to challenge me?"

"What are you?" Alex asked, looking down toward the base of the tower.

Fighting a queasy feeling of worry, Hheilea leaned forward to look down at the speaker. *He's going to be okay. We'll be out of here soon.* A huge, black figure stood in front of the door to the tower. Two big, scaly wings flapped from the figure's back. Even from this distance, Hheilea could see its blazing red eyes. Hheilea's eyes went wide, and she stifled a scream.

The black figure's whip-like tail lashed behind it. A big, toothy grin creased the figure's face. "I'm a gaahr, one of the deem. We are the most powerful creatures of the universe. My name is Gagugugul. You are doomed."

Alex laughed at the pompous statement.

The gaahr stood dressed in only dark-red and gold leather straps. Some areas of its body were blurred by something Hheilea couldn't see. A necklace hung from his neck. *He's twice the size of Alex!*

Momentarily, ropes appeared around the monster, and then disappeared. "You can't defeat me with that kind of trick. I work with the Weird." With a clawed hand, Gagugugul drew a huge sword from a scabbard. "I hope Weldon taught you how to fight with a sword, little boy. I want to have fun defeating you."

Placing a hand on the pommel of his sword, Alex drifted slowly down. The gaahr stretched out his thirty-foot wings and rose to meet him. Alex paused, and Hheilea could hear the uncertainty in his voice as he faced this terror. "I think I'll call you Gargle. How do you know Weldon?"

"We fight together sometimes," Gargle said. "I like him."

Hheilea said in a voice full of concern, "Alex, be careful. You can't trust deems."

Alex glanced up at her and then away.

Gargle laughed. "A young kimley woman, and she has a problem."

"What do you mean?" Alex demanded, moving closer to the deem.

"The Weird knows even if you don't," Gargle said. Lifting his head, he hollered at Hheilea, "A green crystal will help you!"

Alex said, "I thought deems were terrible creatures. You look fearsome but sound quite reasonable."

"Well you see, for now, I'm a tame deem locked inside the computers," Gargle said.

"Then step aside," Alex said, "and I won't have to hurt you."

Gargle laughed. "You insult me by your offer. In this crazy world of the Weird, will fire still burn you?" Then he roared, "I am a deem! I look forward to tasting your flesh."

Alex drifted backwards. "I'm not afraid of you. You sound like a buffoon."

"Then prove it," Gargle said. "Pull your little toothpick out and let's start this dance." He opened his mouth wide and laughed a tremendous bellow of a laugh.

The Weird shouldn't have Alex fighting a deem. He could get seriously hurt. Hheilea tried to communicate with the Weird, but it ignored her.

Below, Alex paused. Squaring his shoulders, he slid his sword out of its scabbard.

Gargle roared and fell back. "The Weird is cheating! It gave you a string-sword."

Hheilea grinned. *Now he should be okay, if he just remembers his training.*

"Who are you?" Alex said in a puzzled tone, but he wasn't looking at Gargle.

Hheilea edged farther out over the edge, trying to see who Alex was talking to.

Alex almost dropped his sword and said out loud in evident confusion, "What's going on?" He tentatively moved into the guard position. His right arm was slightly bent with the sword tip pointed at empty air. The sword glowed along the cutting edge, leaving behind a trail of light as it cut through the air. Alex slashed and stabbed at the air in front of him.

Stunned by his behavior, Hheilea leaned dangerously out from the stone. At the last minute, she pressed her hands against the stone to stop from falling. "What are you doing?"

"What?" Alex stopped to look toward her.

"Look out!" Hheilea and Hymeron shouted at the same

time.

Gargle attacked from below, slashing at Alex's legs.

Alex spun in the air, his feet flipping up over his head. He slashed down with his sword. Light trailed in an arc as the blade descended at the rising Gargle.

Wings beating frantically, Gargle tried to switch course. Now his blade rose in a block against Alex's attack. A ringing "snap" sounded the moment the edge of Alex's sword sliced into and broke off the deem's sword. Gargle threw away the useless stub.

"But he warned me," Alex said. He hung in the air, slowly rotating back to right-side-up.

Gargle circled to Alex's back. Hheilea gasped and tried to shout another warning, but fear for Alex froze her. *Why isn't he attacking the deem?*

Alex shifted his grip to clench his sword and then he moved away from Gargle.

Hymeron yelled, "What are you doing? Gargle's in the other direction!"

Alex swung his sword like a club, bashing at something. The blows stopped as if something in the air blocked them.

"He's fighting someone," Gargle said and laughed, adding, "I think someone's in his mind."

Suddenly, Alex changed direction to charge at Gargle. His sword beat down at the fearsome, black creature.

"You're going to lose. It's been foreseen," Gargle gasped out as he tried to defend himself, but the light-trailing sword bit into his body. Smoke rose each time Alex hit him, with a sizzling sound like a welder cutting through thick metal. Hheilea gasped and her eyes widened at the battle below. One of Gargle's clawed hands ripped Alex's side. Forgetting her location, Hheilea leaned too far forward and lost her balance. She opened her mouth to scream.

~**********~

Hymeron, Alex, and Hheilea stood in the empty Weird room surrounded by white walls. She choked off her scream. A holo field formed around Alex's torso and one arm, as he slumped toward the ground. Hheilea pushing away her disorientation, caught him. She slipped an arm around him and let him lean on her.

"Can we ... get ... out of here?" Alex asked, panting. He coughed and threw up all over Hheilea.

Hymeron backed away from them. "You two need to get cleaned up. We can't leave until the holo field heals your wounds. The Weird doesn't want to get in trouble for letting you leave wounded. In fact, you should see Gursha, or there'll be a scar. What were you doing back there?"

"I, uh ..." Alex paused and said with more confidence, "I fought Gargle and killed him after his claws tore into me ... There was someone or something else."

As he spoke, the splattered liquid disappeared leaving only a faint smell of vomit.

Hheilea said, "After you drew your sword, you asked, 'What's going on?' And you fought something we couldn't see. You weren't fighting Gargle. After Gargle attacked you from below and you fought him off, you stopped and said, 'But he warned me.'"

Alex shook his head. "My memory of the fight's confusing. It's like something was there, but I can't remember clearly. I drew my sword and then ... Then Gargle attacked me from below, and I fought him off and ... charged him. I guess I attacked kind of foolishly. Weldon would've been upset with me."

"What do you mean 'would've?'" Hymeron asked. "He is upset."

"What?" Alex asked. "He wasn't there."

"He's an RE. Of course he was watching," Hymeron said. "He and Gargle are probably talking about the fight right now."

Hheilea grasped Alex's arm. "We better get going. We're supposed to take you to Amable's office after we're done. Don't forget, my name is Hhy and I'm a boy. Never refer to me as Hheilea or as a girl."

Alex looked back at her. "Yes, Hheilea. I mean, Hhy."

Hheilea shook her head at him. "You're hopeless. Try not to do anything stupid."

She started to take a step, but the music temporarily overwhelmed her sense of balance, and she tripped, pulling on Alex. He braced himself and kept her from falling. Breathlessly, she looked up into Alex's blue eyes.

Alex grinned at her. "I'll try not to do anything clumsy either."

Hymeron tugged and yelled at both of them. "Come on! Stop your foolishness!"

Hheilea avoided looking at Alex, as they left the Weird. She considered the months they had spent in the Weird. The human teenager beside her was tanned, obviously stronger, and walked with an assurance born of his experiences. Alex had really worked hard, and the last few days he made amazing progress with his AI. Ahead of her, Hymeron stopped and knocked at Amable's office. Hheilea looked around in surprise.

The door opened, and Amable said, "Come in. Come in."

The three of them stepped through the doorway, and Stick's voice, rising in near panic, greeted Hheilea. "What happened to you? Your shirt's all torn and bloody."

At first, she looked down at her vest in confusion, until she heard Alex speaking from beside her.

"Sorry. I didn't realize how bad it looks. The gaahr injured me at the end of my training."

Amable crowded past Hheilea to snatch Alex's hand and pumped it up and down. "Congratulations on facing a gaahr."

"You should've seen him," Hheilea said proudly. "He finished everything Gursha wanted him to do, and the link he's developed with his AI is already better than what I can do. The AI itself is changing and growing to meet his demands."

Amable beamed. "Of course Alex did great. He's quite the boy."

Alex stood still for a second. "Uh, yeah. I really wasn't that great." Changing the topic, he asked, "What's the rest of the flock doing now?"

"Today was their third day in the Hall of Flight," Amable answered.

"But," Alex said. "Their first day was months ago."

Amable laughed. "You've a lot to learn, Alex. Only three

days have passed for us. You and the kimley kids have been in a time bubble."

"A time ...," Alex began and instead asked, "What should I do now?"

"Your clothes are a great badge of courage, but get them changed and have a late lunch with the kimleys. Then come back here," Amable said.

Hheilea let the boys lead the way to lunch. She remained quiet, absorbed in her own thoughts. *The music isn't stopping. I shouldn't be hearing it around Alex. He's a human and only a boy. What's going to happen?*

Chapter Nine
T'wasn't-to-be-is

Hheilea walked down the corridor on the way back from lunch. She kept looking at Alex. *He should've listened to me.*

Hymeron snickered and said, "Hheilea told you the spicy, lillyputi dessert can be addictive."

Sweat ran down Alex's face. "I can't forget it. I need more." He stopped to sniff the air. Grasping his shirt, he jerked it to his mouth, and sucked on a spot where the dessert had spilled, and sighed with pleasure.

Hheilea took Alex's arm and began urging him on toward Amable's office. At first, Alex let her, but after a couple of steps, he slowed and looked back the way they had come.

She tugged at Alex's arm but couldn't get him to move. "I need your help, Hymeron. If we can get him to Amable's office, he can use *state of mind* to remove the addictive effects."

Alex leaned away from them. "Come on. Let me go back for seconds."

Hymeron tugged on Alex's hand. "I think that dessert will need to be placed on the restricted list for humans."

"Amable's office is just a few feet farther," Hheilea said, struggling to keep Alex moving the right way.

Hymeron kicked at the door, and it slid open.

Hheilea hung from Alex's hand, her feet dragging, as Alex walked back the way they had come. "Amable, we need some help."

"I'm coming," Amable said.

Alex dragged her and Hymeron back down the passageway. From behind them came Amable's voice. "What's

73

going on?"

"Alex ate some lillyputi dessert," Hheilea said. "He's trying to go back."

Alex said, "I've got to have more."

Amable said, "It's my favorite dessert too."

Still getting dragged backward, Hheilea snapped, "Amable!"

Amable said, "Yes. Just relax, Alex. We all love you. Everything is going to be fine."

Alex slowly stopped dragging the kimleys. He glanced down at them with a confused expression. "What just happened?"

"You had an addictive reaction to a dessert," Hymeron said. "Amable helped by calming you."

Alex looked even more confused.

Amable gestured toward his office. "Come into my office and I'll explain."

Approaching the office, Alex began to hear a song playing. "Where's the music coming from?"

Once in the office, Amable pointed to a plant occupying one corner of the room. Its leaves were large, translucent, filled with liquid, and had fish-like creatures swimming in them.

Hheilea stopped. *More music I don't want to hear.* "Is it just starting to play the ode? I don't want to be here for it."

Amable brushed some dust off his clothes. "The Ode of Remembrance finished playing a little while ago. Now about what I did, you'll learn one of the effects from exposure to Dark Matter can be the ability to change the state of another creature's mind. The more you care for them the better it works. I can encourage others around me to be at peace. I did that for your mind."

Hheilea watched Alex who gazed with wide eyes at Amable. In response, Amable waggled his bushy eyebrows and chuckled. "I suppose you're wondering if I can hypnotize you. The answer is no. There is a more enslaving way of affecting someone else's mind. You'll learn about it in the Controlling Animals class."

Amable looked at each of them. "Alex, earlier, the boys

gave me a glowing report of your training. Was there anything you would like to add? Did anything ... out of the ordinary happen?"

Alex's mouth opened, shut, and then he said, "When I drew the sword to fight the gaahr, Hymeron and Hhei— say I started acting strange and fought something they couldn't see."

"Can you remember—?" Amable gave a sigh and opened a drawer in his desk. "Gursha wants to see you this evening. Work with her to figure out this mystery and give me a call if you need help. For now, take the afternoon off. The boys can show you around. Your flock leader, Ytell, will be in touch with you sometime today."

"How will I call you? I don't think my cell phone works here." Alex said.

Amable paused his rummaging in the drawer to look at Alex and laugh. "Cell phone? Oh, that's a good joke. Contact me through your AI. If you want to talk to me, just think, 'I need to talk to Amable.' Most of us have some form of AI. Stick's AI is how he interfaces with the files and the paperwork he's always working with. Everyone from Earth is receiving their own AI." Amable pulled a disc from the drawer. "Good, here it is. Hymeron, take this with you just in case Alex has a relapse of his addiction. Just aim the pointy end at him and push this button. He'll lose consciousness for a little while. It isn't dangerous, but make sure you don't play with it, and bring it back tomorrow."

Hymeron took the small disc. "Great, this will be fun. See ya."

Hheilea said, "Is it a good idea to give him a stunner?" She could imagine Hymeron running through the corridors stunning everyone.

Amable grinned in response. "Have you heard the saying, 'Give a man enough rope and he'll hang himself?' Consider this another test for you and your brother. If I hear any reports of people falling unconscious, I'll know who to blame and will have no qualms about restricting the two of you to your quarters. Besides, Alex really might have a relapse in the next few hours."

Hheilea scowled. "I wouldn't trust Hymeron with it. You should've given it to me. It's going to be your fault if something goes wrong. Come on, Alex, let's go."

"I'll be with you in a second," Alex said. "Amable?"

"Yes, my boy?"

"Did you know something strange is going on with me?"

Hheilea heard the beginning of the conversation as she left. Concern for Alex slowed her footsteps, but she resolutely continued on. *I need to respect his privacy.* Hymeron stopped to listen, and she whispered, "Come on," and gave him her big sister glare.

Hymeron shrugged and continued with her. After a while, they heard Alex jogging after them. "Sorry I took so long. Let's go see my flock."

"You just want to see A'idah," Hymeron said with a grin as they waited for Alex.

"What?" Alex asked with an innocent expression, as he caught up.

Hymeron elbowed him. "I saw you look all googly-eyed at her in the clinic."

Hheilea bit her lip at the conversation.

Alex said, "No, not me. Well, maybe some at first. You know it's been very confusing for me. Okay, that was lame. You know she's much younger than me. I think she's only twelve, and I'm fifteen. What about you? How old are you?"

"I'm ten," Hymeron said and added, emphasizing the first three words, "and my brother is eleven. In the next five years, I'll make all the decisions for my adult life."

Hheilea scowled, looking down at her feet. She didn't like this lying to Alex. *I'm actually about the same age as Alex. Except I'll be an adult this year, and he's going to continue just being a teenager.*

Alex looked at Hymeron. "Really? You guys don't seem that young. Why would you make those decisions so young?"

Hheilea spoke quickly before she could change her mind. "When we turn fifteen, we eventually start hearing a song. It's the beginning of our becoming adults. We're adults and almost always married before we are sixteen." Bitterly she added, "Then we lose touch with *now*."

"But why am I hearing—." Alex started to ask, and then he said, "No way. I'd be getting married soon, and I'm way too young for that. What do you mean 'losing touch with now?'"

Hymeron said, "You need to meet our family. I'm warning you, for most people it's a crazy experience."

Hheilea walked along with them, stealing looks at Alex. Occasionally, she caught him looking at her. Neither one said anything. The song, crashing of waves on a distant shore and tinkling of wind chimes, mesmerized her, until she walked into a corner of the corridor. She tried to regain control. It helped when she saw Alex doing the same thing. He looked away from Hheilea, and she laughed to herself, breathing deep. The confusion was still there, but something else, a feeling of rightness, began to grow. *But he's so young.* Hymeron stopped at the door to their home. A red haze settled over them, and a voice asked, "Are you intending or planning any harm to this family?"

"No," both kimleys said, and then they looked at Alex.

"No. I'm not," Alex said, truthfully.

The voice said as the door slid open, "You are cleared to enter, but an anomalous reading for Alex is noted in the records."

Stepping into the room, Hheilea looked around and for the first time felt self-conscious about her home. *How does Alex see all of this?* The colors of the walls flowed from one to another. A stack of different-sized bowls rested on the top of a green, three-foot tall column. Several other columns with stacks of things, a table on the other side, and three chairs filled the room. Hheilea looked at everything and then at Alex. He gazed open-mouthed at everything. Her dad, his multicolored hair shimmering like butterfly wings, walked out of a passageway. He didn't look at them. Instead, he looked back the way he came, yelling, "Hymeron, leave your sister alone!" Almost covered by shoulder-length hair, a green lizard stood on his shoulder, looking at them with jewel-like eyes. The man turned back toward the doorway and shouted, "Don't do that!"

"Alex, meet my dad. Dad, this is Alex," Hymeron said.

"He was happy to meet you," the lizard on the man's

shoulder said.

Alex held his hand out in greeting, but the man didn't respond. "Why is he yelling at you two and you're not even where he's yelling?"

"He's responding to some future, maybe not even one that will come to pass. Lately, Dad has been worse than normal. It's like he overdosed on lillyputi dessert."

The man hurried to the bowls and grabbed one out of the middle of the stack, leaving the bowls above it hovering in the air. The hovering bowls slowly settled down onto those below. Meanwhile, the man walked across the room and held the bowl at the edge of the table. The only thing on the table was a pedestal, with a pile of beads on it. After a moment, he put the bowl back. The stack of bowls adjusted itself to accept the bowl back into the stack.

"Over there's my mom," Hymeron said, pointing past a cluster of columns with their stacks.

Alex raised his hand in greeting to the woman, but she just sat still, not looking at him. Hymeron walked into the room and slipped the bottom bowl off the column.

"Why's she just sitting?" Alex asked Hheilea. "And what's up with the lizards?"

Hheilea turned a sad expression to Alex. "Mom shared too much of what she sees in the future. That made her view of the future so chaotic, she almost went catatonic. She's getting better."

"The lizards are cadleys. We all have them. When we're young, they come and go, but after our fourteenth birthday, they stay with us most of the time. It's a symbiotic relationship. We provide a safe place with food and they help us with living in the now."

Hheilea moved her hair out of the way, and a bright green cadley scampered out of Hheilea's white hair. "Here, meet Neet. When I'm out in public, Neet has to stay hidden. We don't want anyone to know how old I am."

Neet tipped her head back and forth looking at Alex, and Hheilea said, "Hold your hand out."

On the other side of the room Hymeron set the bowl on a chair below the edge of the table and then sat down and rested his head on the table.

Alex held his hand out, and Neet jumped onto it and scampered up to his shoulder.

Neet asked Hheilea, |Can I taste his ear wax?|

Alex's eyes snapped wide open.

Hheilea said, "What?"

"I heard something in my mind. A voice whispered to me," Alex said.

Hheilea's expression changed to one of wonder and amazement. "You shouldn't have heard that. No one but a kimley can hear cadleys' telepathy, and their thoughts are heard by only a cadley's symbiotic partner or the mate of its partner. Neet asked me if she could taste your earwax. It's a delicacy for them."

The tinkling of wind chimes rising and falling like waves on a shore rose to a roar in her mind. Distracted by the music, she almost didn't hear Alex's answer.

"Yeah, sure." And then Alex grinned. "She's tickling me."

Hheilea took Neet back. *I have to go get dressed for the t'wasn't-to-be-is. My time has come.* All her confusion disappeared. She looked intently at Alex and spoke firmly. "Wait here."

Quickly, she ran to her room. Eagerly, she tore off her clothes and pulled a beautiful white dress from her closet. With fluid movements, she slipped it on. Leaving her room, she spotted the t'wasn't-to-be plant. The strange plant grew in an oval glass pot filled with water. At the base of the pot was the seed the plant grew from. The plant grew up into a circle with a bloom, and dangling down from the bloom, the seed the plant grew from. As she looked, flesh of a fruit rapidly started covering the seed.

Alex stood gazing at the plant too, and he said in a dream-like voice, "What's that?"

A panicked Hymeron said to Alex, "Get out of here!"

Hheilea hurried out of the passageway and brushed past Hymeron. She could see the confusion in his face. *I wish my little brother wasn't so confused about Alex and me. My t'wasn't-to-be-is ceremony is wonderful.*

Mesmerized by the music, Hheilea stepped to the beat

that rhythmically pulled her toward Alex. Her gaze locked on his blue eyes. She felt herself drowning in them as she stepped toward him. She reached for him. Their hands touched, and the world around her disappeared.

Chapter Ten
Control

Blinking, Alex struggled to sit up, and then he laid back down as vertigo threatened his consciousness. Light brown walls surrounded him and Hymeron. "What happened?"

Hymeron stood, back to the door, glaring at Alex. He pointed down at Alex. "You idiot. You began to dance the t'wasn't-to-be-is dance with my sister. What do you remember?"

Irritation at Hymeron's words and aggressive tone cleared the fog in Alex's mind. "A figure coming toward me. It was Hheilea. She was so beautiful. And then ... I don't remember any more. Where is she?"

"She's resting. She's an idiot too. What were you thinking? You shouldn't be dancing the t'wasn't-to-be-is dance with her."

"Get out of my face, Hymeron. Back off. I didn't dance it on purpose."

"Maybe you didn't you—, but the result's the same. I stopped you. I used the device Amable gave me to knock the two of you out."

Alex struggled to get up. "You what?!"

Hymeron stepped closer, getting in the way of Alex getting up. "I knocked both of you out. I carried Hheilea back to her room, and I dragged you to this storage room. I was lucky no one saw me in the passageway."

Alex shoved against Hymeron's legs. *This fool stole something from me. The music and Hheilea are both wonderful.* "I tried to get you and Hheilea to explain about the music I was hearing during the last months, but you wouldn't.

81

You kept ignoring me and saying I was imagining things. I knew Hheilea was hearing it too. How did it force me into the dance with Hheilea? What is this dance?" Other questions he didn't want to ask Hymeron filled his mind. *Where is Hheilea? I want to be with her. What's happening to me?*

"The dance marks the beginning of two kimleys' transition to adulthood. We say the music is their future calling to them and bringing them together. Those who dance together ... I don't know why or how you're caught up in this. It's wrong! You can't dance the t'wasn't-to-be-is."

Alex winced at the forcefulness of Hymeron's voice. "What does 't'wasn't-to-be-is' mean?"

Hymeron leaned over Alex, still glaring and breathing hard. He closed his eyes and began speaking as if from rote. "T'wasn't-to-be-is speaks of the adult life the kimley participants are moving into and uses a mix of tenses we are familiar with. Adults live in multiple possible futures. They experience the future in their present tense, but the thing is they can experience futures that probably can't happen. Those futures are called by my people, 'it-was-not-to-be' or 'twasn't-to-be'. Sometimes, the twasn't-to-be future ends up happening and therefore is. That future has become a t'wasn't-to-be-is. There's a legend among my people. It says our whole species is working to make a future a long time away, which is extremely unlikely, happen. It is called the 't'wasn't-to-be-is legend.' The term also refers to what you started to experience."

"Thanks. I understand better," Alex said. *How can they live in the future? What's it like?*

"We need to get you back to your flock," Hymeron said, as Alex opened his mouth to ask another question. "Don't tell others about this and don't go looking for Hheilea."

Alex began to stand up when Hymeron pushed against his shoulder shoving him down.

"Stop," Hymeron said.

Alex froze, clenching his hands, and growled, "Now what's wrong?" *I'm going to beat ...*

Hymeron started rubbing at Alex's hair. Instead of angry, now his voice was frantic. "It won't come off."

"Stop that! What won't come off?"

Sitting back with a stunned expression, Hymeron looked into Alex's eyes, and then he tipped his head to the side. "See the iridescent scales on the skin of my temples?"

"Yeah. What about them?"

"When I start to become an adult, those scales move from my temples into my hair and I'll end up looking like my dad with iridescent colors shimmering as my hair moves."

At first, Alex didn't understand, then his mouth dropped open, and he frantically looked about the room, hoping to find something he could see his hair in.

"It shouldn't be," Hymeron said. "The hair on your temples is starting to get the fine scales that will give your hair the color of my dad."

"No! Oh, no. I'm going to look like your dad?"

"My dad looks good."

Alex took a deep breath. He could really use Amable and his ability to calm others. *This is too strange. I'm just a teenager and a human. I'm not an alien.*

Hymeron continued speaking, "You have to stay here. I'm going to figure out a plan to deal with you."

"No!" Alex shot to his feet and shoved Hymeron against the wall. "You are not going to make any plans for me. I've had it with everyone and everything controlling me. I'm going to take care of this."

Hymeron stared back and Alex looked down to see Hymeron pulling the stunner out of his pocket. With one hand Alex grabbed Hymeron by the throat and slammed him against the wall. With the other he struggled to tear the device from Hymeron's hand. Gasping and clawing with his free hand the kimley fought back, but Alex's training both with the kimleys and with Twarbie had endowed him with superior strength. It only took him a few moments to pull the disc from Hymeron. Then remembering Amable's instructions, he pointed it at Hymeron and pushed the button. Instantly Hymeron collapsed.

Alex backed up against a wall and slid to the floor. *I'm free. Yeah about as free as a moth in a spider web. How was I forced into the t'wasn't-be thing?* Alex tried not to think

83

about Hheilea. *I can't be rational if I think of her.* Then his thoughts lurched to Twarbie and the secret time he'd spent with her. *I can't believe how I've grown to care for her.* The memory of their kisses burned in his mind and the music playing in his head died away. *It's not her choice to be terrible. She wants to be different and I want to help her, but she slammed the door on that possibility.* He ground his teeth at the memory of her warning. Hearing her voice again and almost smelling her fragrance. "Don't try and find me or help me. Remember if the other winkles know you're my friend, then they'll force me to torture you to death and I can't stand that thought. I'll just be how I'm expected to be."

Bashing his fist against the floor. He muttered to himself. "Twarbie might think she had no choice, but I do and I don't give up." In a moment he jumped to his feet and left the room.

When Alex shut the door of the storage room behind him he paused for only a second before thinking of Gursha and hoped she could help him with his strange hair. After that he would have to take things one step at a time. No matter what, he vowed, he would stay in control. Alex remembered what he'd told Peter. "This is a chance for us to help other people." *One thing I know, it won't be easy. I've got so many problems, and I'm just getting started.* The words of his father came to Alex. We *all need help with the little we have, to do what we can.*

An Author's Note

I hope you've enjoyed the novella 'Alex Twice Abducted' as much as I enjoyed creating it for you. In a novella it's impossible to show the richness of a novel. In the following pages are three excerpts. The first is from the novel '*Alex and inner voice.*' The rest are from the last novel of this series '*Alex and the Crystal of Jedh.*' At this date the last novel is still being edited, so there will be some changes. These excerpts will give you a glimpse of the rest of this series and the world of the dark universe series. The scenes are chosen to fit a movie trailer design.

In the first you meet four friends you've already read about and hear the voice of Maleky speaking in Alex's head. You'll see them in a most interesting situation.

First Excerpt

While Alex slept, a breeze blew through the open window. In the twilight a slight figure with shoulder length white hair climbed into Alex and Zeghes' bedroom. The person shook Alex and in a quiet voice said, "Wake up, Alex."

Alex groaned and rolled over.

Zeghes slowly undulating in the air on the other side of the room said, "Hello. Who are you?"

Then he answered himself. "You're one of the kimley boys, except you're not a boy. Why does everyone call you a boy?"

Alex groggily said, "What's going on?

At the same time Hheilea let out a surprised and slightly indignant denial. "I am too a boy."

Zeghes twisted in the air and swung his head back and forth. "Your body's different from Alex's and he's a boy. Your body's very similar to A'idah's and she's a girl."

"How do you know that?" Hheilea said, stepping back from Zeghes.

Zeghes swung his head back and forth. "When I move my head I'm looking at you carefully."

Awakened by the conversation, Alex sat up in bed. "He uses sound to be able to see in the water and it works in the air."

"But... But... my clothes—," Hheilea began to protest and Zeghes cut her off. "I can see through clothing very easily."

"Ahhh!" Hheilea ducked down behind Alex's bed.

"What is it about clothing? I don't wear any," Zeghes said in annoyance, swatting his tail against the air.

Hheilea stayed squatted down, arms crossed over her chest. "I'm used to seeing some species without clothes, but I'm not used to having someone look right through my clothing. I'm sorry Zeghes. My reaction must seem silly to you."

Slowly she stood up. Even in the dim, early morning light Alex could see the blush. "Zeghes, this is Hheilea. She's Hymeron's older sister. Please keep calling her Hhy. Kimleys are always in danger in our galaxy from individuals who act like sharks. Girls Hheilea's age are in even more danger.

That's why she's supposed to be in disguise as a younger boy. Can you help us keep her secret?"

"I'll protect you from the sharks," Zeghes said.

"Thanks, Zeghes," Hheilea said.

Alex looked at Hheilea. "What are you doing in here?"

"I needed to talk to you, but it's after five in the morning now. You'll have your alibi."

In a moment Hheilea climbed back out the window and was gone, leaving Alex puzzled about her alibi stuff as he quickly fell back to sleep.

Later, Alex stumbled into the cafeteria looking for something to wake him up. A'idah sat at a small table by herself, her head in her hands. Zeghes swam past Alex and said to him, "You don't look like you got enough sleep with Hheilea waking you up early this morning."

Startled, his grogginess shed, Alex started to speak. *He isn't supposed to use her real name. Someone's going to hear.*

A'idah looked up.

From behind Alex, Hheilea said, "Good morning."

Zeghes said, "Good morning, Hheilea."

Maleky yelled in Alex's head. Stop him! Don't let people know her name! And he continued to yell comments and instructions as the conversation continued around Alex.

"Zeghes, you aren't supposed to—," Alex began to say.

A'idah interrupted Alex. "Hheilea? Aren't you Hhy? One of the Soaley boys."

Alex hurried toward A'idah as he hissed. "Zeghes, come here." Reaching a puzzled A'idah, Alex continued talking. "A'idah, Hhy is Hheilea in disguise. All of the kimleys are in danger, but girls who are about to become women are in extreme danger."

A'idah jumped to her feet, knocking over her table, and in a moment she hugged Hheilea and then turned back to glare at Zeghes and Alex. "We have to protect her. Zeghes, you can't say her real name where anyone,"

Alex stepped back at the intensity in A'idah's voice as she continued. "and I mean anyone, but us or her family might hear."

Zeghes came close and touched Hheilea with his beak. "I

thought it was okay to share secrets within the pod."

A tear ran down A'idah's face as she muttered to herself. "It isn't going to happen this time." In a commanding voice she continued, "We can't risk her secret with anyone else." A'idah loosened her arm's hold around Hheilea just enough to switch to holding her with both of her hands by the shoulders and spoke directly to Hheilea. "Who's the danger to you? Why are you in danger?" She finished with an emphatic statement, not waiting for any answers. "I'm not going to let anyone hurt you."

Second Excerpt

In the second snapshot are three sections. These are all from the last novel in this series, '*Alex and the Crystal of Jedh.*' This novel is still being edited so there might be some changes. You see more of Hheilea the kimley, almost a woman by her species, and A'idah, a 12 year old Kalasha girl. She's considered a woman by some of the followers of the religion her father belongs to. With these three sections we glimpse some of the struggles the girls fight in the story.

First Section

A'idah waved a hand and shouted. "Over here, Hhy."

Hheilea waved back and slogged her way through the despondent groups of Earthlings. A'idah turned to the Palestinian boy and said, "Help me make the table bigger."

Both of them grasped the round table by the edge and pulled. The table responded by stretching to double its original size.

Hheilea scooted a chair over to their table. "I saw Alex go to the Gadget Lady. He'll be back later today."

Momentarily the welcome news pushed aside the unidentified gloom surrounding A'idah. "I'm glad his months of effort to get to her are paying off. I can hardly wait to see what he brings back." The gloom surged back. "I doubt if your good news will make any difference." She waved her hand. "Look at everyone. It's as if we're all waiting for some impending doom to strike."

Hheilea sat down. "I know. We need to be getting things done, but everyone is moving at half speed and not getting anything done. How about you? Have you made any progress solving your problem?"

A'idah frowned. "No. Socra and Tease said I should go see the Grand Imam of the Academy, but trying to make the right decision seems so hopeless."

Hheilea moved closer and grasped A'idah's hand. "Remember what those two women told us about hope being available for all if we are just willing to accept it. Being stuck in indecision is like standing still in the path of an onrushing deem. You have to make a decision. Standing still is a certain recipe for disaster."

"I know," A'idah said bitterly. "I'm being an idiot."

"Let's go and see the Imam then. Come on. I'll go with you," Hheilea said.

A'idah angrily jerked herself to her feet, knocking over her chair. "You're right. I'm being stupid. Let's go."

Second Section

Hheilea stopped her from getting on a yellow circle by herself. "Let's ride in a bubble together and have the boys go ahead of us. Then we can talk."

"Great idea."

The girls followed the boys' two bubbles floating over the sea. All the way, Hheilea kept quiet, answering A'idah in short sentences. Getting annoyed, A'idah stared at her. Hheilea looked anywhere except at A'idah.

A'idah grasped Hheilea's head and growled. "Look at me."

Tears began to trickle down Hheilea's cheeks.

A'idah dropped her hands. Frustration filled her voice, as she asked, "What's wrong? You ask me to ride with you so we can talk, and you don't talk, and now you're crying?"

"Your friend... who died.... You almost died trying to save her."

"I wish I had saved her even if it meant I died doing it." It still hurt A'idah to talk about it. She looked at Hheilea. A suspicion began to grow in her mind. "Are you worried about what I'll do to try and save you?"

Hheilea vigorously nodded her head up and down. Tears flew off her cheeks to land on the wall of the bubble and course down the sides. "My dad said I need to talk to you. This is part of my secret. I can talk to my dad and he can tell me things from the future. It's because of the position I'm stuck in with Alex and the 'twasn't-tobe-is'. Dad said—."

Tears and a sob interfered with her efforts to talk.

A'idah took her in her arms and held her close. Fiercely, she said, "I failed to save my other friend. If I fail to save you, I don't want to live."

"Why?"

Knocking a tear off her own cheek with a fist, A'idah answered. "I am free to do what I choose. I chose to save my friend and now I choose to save you. If I fail again, it will be too much. What's the use of being free to choose, if you can't succeed?" *But I don't want to die.*

Third Section

The man smiled at A'idah. "You have the spirit of Nusayba. May you also defend Muhammad, God's peace and blessings be upon him. Others have already asked about your situation. And I say to you what I said to them. It is not your menses alone that shows your maturity for the commitment to observe prayer and fasting as a Muslim. Allah Almighty says: 'Prove orphans till they reach the marriageable age; then if you find them of sound judgment, deliver them over unto them their fortune.' I am quoting a fatwa from An-Nisa. I would not force you to follow your father's beliefs, but encourage you to consider the results of your choices as you learn sound judgment. In this, I am supported by other previous fatwas such as one by Muhammad 'Ali Al-Hanooti back on Earth. May Allah guide us all to the straight path and direct us to that which pleases Him Amen.

The younger man coughed and everyone looked at him. "My esteemed father gives you the best answer he can, but I say you are already over nine lunar years old. Yes?"

A'idah felt a chill run down her spine. "Yes."

The man nodded, his hair fell forward and back. "Then by the example of Muhammad, God's peace and blessings be upon him, you have reached the age of Taklig and are mature. If you're not living as a Muslim you're an Apostate. Now here we don't kill Apostates, but on this last part my father and I agree. When you return to Earth you'll face those who will believe if you are an Apostate you should be punished by death.

The rest of the visit passed as a blur for A'idah. She remembered saying, "Thank you."

On the way back up to the surface Hheilea and A'idah traveled together. Hheilea asked, "Did that help?"

Third Excerpt

The third excerpt is also in three sections. These are all from the last novel in this series, '*Alex and the Crystal of Jedh.*' This novel is still being edited so there might be some changes. These are separate excerpts from fights.

First Section

Alex heard the little lizard-like creature, the cadley, sadly say, "Goodbye. It was nice knowing you."

A limp sensation followed behind the cold. *I can't move. What did it mean? Am I going to die?* Alex watched the ground passing. He sped past a big, hinged metal door set flat into the ground. *At least I can see.* His body rotated from the wind blasting past. A gaahr by the crystal turned toward him. *I'm going to crash into him.* AI, stop us. Alex felt gravity pull him to a stop. At the same moment the cadley sprang off toward the gaahr. The gaahr pointed a hand at Alex and said, "Die."

Alex's hair stood up on end. AI, Alex screamed in his mind, get us out of here. Alex felt movement and heard an explosion in-between him and the gaahr. The blast knocked Alex back. Blazing light and the boom of thunder dazed Alex. Dimly he thought to AI, use no set path. Go up, down, forward and backward. Move fast. His view spun. Jerks to his body testified to changes in direction, as the AI on his skull followed his directions. The music and words sounded anew in Alex's head. The song of the island battled past his thoughts and feelings.

Don't wait, our death comes. I come. We're doomed. Where can we run?

Never give up. Death crashes down. Tomorrow we see the sun.

A ball of fire roared past. More lightning struck. Alex tried to figure out what just happened. *The cadley told me goodbye. It jumped toward the gaahr. Then an explosion pushed me away just before the lightning strike. Did the cadley die saving me? But why?* AI, keep moving us, but use the same gravity generators to pull my sword out.

I can do that, AI answered. This is fun. I like moving things using artificial gravity.

Second Section

Alex commanded his AI to throw the sword like a spear at the gaahr. He heard again his plea set to the music of the island.

I will not let you be killed. I'll stop evil. I'll save you.
What is our future? Can I be true? Who knows? Who?

He heard a distant agonizing scream. His heart broke within. He whispered "No."

Third Section

The gaahr turned on Alex. With a massive hand he drew a long black sword. Guttural words blasted out of his huge maw. "Puny boy, you'll die for this."

Alex told AI, bring my sword back. The sword whistled through the air. Both the gaahr and Alex ducked as it flew past. Bring it carefully to my hand so I can grasp the grip.

Sorry, AI responded. I'm a little excited. When can I fly more stuff around?

The gaahr said, "Hurry up and get your fancy toothpick and we'll get this dance going." He added with a laugh, his fangs dripping. "It won't last long."

Alex caught his sword. "You sound like another gaahr I know. You're right this fight will end quickly." *He must not know I have a string-sword from the Gadget Lady. My sword will cut through anything except dark matter.*

"I am Hagabagaga. Prepare to die."

It's the gaahr from the class. Working with AI, Alex flew through the air. Hagabagaga came to meet him. The Gaahr's black sword slashed down. Alex swung his sword over his head. The edge of his sword trailed white light as it rose to meet the other sword. He expected to slice through Hagabagaga's sword. The resulting blow of sword on sword almost tore Alex's sword from his grasp. Instead, it forced him back and down.

TLW Savage, Author

Tim lives in his RV and is now an Idahoan. He's actually Tim Walker. Savage is an old family name, and he decided to start using it to make it easier for fans to differentiate him from other authors.

A grandpa, he and his wife enjoy their children and grandchildren. He loves making great food and gets even more enjoyment from watching family and friends eat the food.

He began creating stories at an early age. One night his seven-year-old sister woke screaming, and he went to comfort her. On the spur of the moment, the twelve-year-old Tim created a fantastical story for her, calming her with attention grabbing details. He still remembers that story. Tim has an even earlier memory of creating a story sometime between six and seven-years-old, but he doesn't remember much of that incident.

Tim has one more book he's working on for this series. It's called Alex and the Crystal of Jedh. Next, he's working on four other books in the same story line. They will be set back on Earth. He's going to explore the location, a remote mountain range called Henry's mountains in south-eastern Utah. They are a fascinating place with many interesting plants and animals. The geology is unique. He'll be going back to Henry's mountains a number of times to get the details of those stories right.

Tim's fascinated by everything from flowers to Genghis Kahn and sand to Mount Everest. He finds people particularly interesting and is always on the watch for interesting features and personality quirks. If you come to his website and visit, you might find yourself in a book. He's active in local writing groups and is a beta reader for other writers. You can find him at:

tlwalkerauthor.com or his new website tlwsavageauthor.com

Contact the Author

I would love to hear back from my fans. Please contact me at my email: tlwalker@twalkerauthor.com. Plus, if you provide me with a suggestion, such as a type of animal or a scene, and I use it, I will then include your name on the acknowledgment page. Also, for my younger fans if you take the book to school and your whole class makes a suggestion and I use it, then I will include the whole class, everyone's name, on a special page just for them. Remember the simpler the suggestion the easier and more likely I will use it. Thanks for being a fan. I hope to see you someday at a book signing.

Author Visit

Tim has started doing author visits at schools. He loves doing them and wants to do more. Contact his agent Laura Barr at (360) 584-4241, email laurambarr91@gmail.com.

Made in the USA
Middletown, DE
10 June 2019